Mills & Boon
Best Seller Romance

A chance to read and collect some of the best-loved novels from Mills & Boon—the world's largest publisher of romantic fiction.

Every month, six titles by favourite Mills & Boon authors will be re-published in the *Best Seller Romance* series.

A list of other titles in the *Best Seller Romance* series can be found at the end of this book.

SARA CRAVEN
WILD MELODY

MILLS & BOON LIMITED
LONDON · TORONTO

First published 1977
Australian copyright 1983
Philippine copyright 1983
This edition 1983

© Sara Craven 1977

ISBN 0 263 74257 1

Set in Monotype Plantin 10 on 11 pt.
02–0483

Made and printed in Great Britain by
Richard Clay (The Chaucer Press) Ltd,
Bungay, Suffolk

CHAPTER ONE

'LASSIE, are you sure?' Mrs McGregor, her ample form wrapped securely in a flowered pinny, paused in her task of kneading dough, and stared at the slight figure on the other side of the big kitchen table.

'Quite sure,' Catriona Muir said, with a firmness she was far from feeling. 'I—I simply must get away. The Mackintoshes want vacant possession as soon as possible, and now the house is sold, I feel as if I don't belong there anyway.'

'Don't belong?' Mrs McGregor attacked the dough with renewed vigour. 'Away with you! In your own aunt's house where you were brought up as a bairn?'

'The Mackintoshes own it now,' Catriona reminded her with a pang. It still hurt to think of it. The big grey house standing back from the road had been home as long as she could remember. Ever since, in fact, the parents who were just vague pictures in her mind had been killed in a car crash and Auntie Jessie, her father's unmarried sister and Catriona's only living relative, had descended on her and carried her back to the tiny village of Torvaig on the west coast of Scotland.

Now, eighteen years later, Aunt Jessie too was dead, and Muir House—surely, as she herself had ruefully said, the most unsuccessful guest-house in Scotland—had been sold to a Glasgow couple.

'Aye, they own it,' Mrs McGregor retorted. 'But for how long?' She dropped the dough back into its bowl. 'If a fine woman like Jessie Muir couldn'a make the place pay, then it's no likely that painted besom and her man will do any better. This is the wrong place for summer boarders, my dear, and that's the truth of it. We're too far away from Fort William and the Islands and the things folk come to see. It's a family house, that. It's crying out for bairns and laughter, and it'll no take kindly to that one and her—improvements.' Mrs McGregor invested the last word with incredible scorn. 'A discothèque in the basement! Have you ever heard such nonsense?'

Catriona smiled unhappily. 'I think she's being a little un-realistic.'

'And so are you.' Mrs McGregor folded her arms and gazed at Catriona sternly. 'Chasing off to England after some laddie that's never given you a thought all year.'

Catriona flushed and her green eyes grew stormy.

'That's not true,' she protested. 'Jeremy didn't come this spring, I know, but he has written to me.'

'Not for several months he hasn't,' retorted Mrs Mc-Gregor with all the calm assurance of the sister of the village postmistress. 'And don't jut that Muir chin at me, my lass. There's no one in this village with anything but your good at heart, and they'd all tell you what I'm telling you now. A few moonlight kisses by the sea-loch don't make a marriage.'

She nodded emphatically at Catriona, whose cheeks were flaming.

'Och, we've all been through it, lassie,' she went on kindly. 'First love's a grand thing, but it doesn't last. When it's real love, you'll know, just as I knew with Mr McGregor.'

Catriona looking at the round plump face with its coronet of wispy grey hair and visualising the balding taciturn Mr McGregor had to repress a desire to giggle, in spite of her annoyance. What did Mrs McGregor know of the sweet and tender secret she and Jeremy had shared in that magical few weeks the previous year when he had come to Torvaig on a walking tour and stayed and stayed until his time was up, and he had to return to university?

6

Thinking of Jeremy with his crisp dark hair and laughing blue eyes brought a tightening to her throat and a mistiness to her eyes. They had shared so much. They had walked, sailed and swum during those golden days that seemed as if they would last for ever.

One night they had attended a *ceilidh* in a neighbouring village. Catriona, who played the guitar and sang folk songs in English and Gaelic, had been one of the star turns, and later as they drove home in the back of Angus Duncan's van along the narrow single track road with the clumps of grass growing in the centre which was Torvaig's only means of access with the outside world, Jeremy had drawn her close.

'I never knew you could sing like that,' he whispered, his lips against her ear.

Catriona, more used to her aunt's affectionate bluntness and the villagers' forthrightness, had blushed.

'Oh, it's nothing,' she said awkwardly.

'Nothing!' Jeremy cast his eyes to heaven. 'My love, in London you'd be a hit. You've got real talent, and you don't even know it. The record companies are always crying out for something new, and those songs you sang in that outlandish language . . .'

'The Gaelic is not outlandish!' Catriona flared. 'And I wish I could speak it properly instead of just being able to sing a few songs in it.'

'Okay, okay,' Jeremy said placatingly. 'But it does sound strange when you're not used to it. I think that with the proper backing and promotion you could be Scotland's answer to Nana Mouskouri.'

'I'd be more flattered if I knew who she was,' Catriona said, resting her head sleepily on his shoulder.

'Seriously, Trina,' he put his fingers under her chin, forcing her to look up at him, 'you shouldn't waste yourself in this wilderness. You'd have far more chance in London.'

'Wilderness?' Catriona faced him bewilderedly. 'But, Jeremy, I thought you liked Torvaig.'

'I do like it,' he said. 'But I like it because you're here. Without you, I wouldn't have spent a second day here. It's too quiet for me. I like some action.'

Remembering this now in the homely warmth of the McGregor kitchen, Catriona felt her spirits plummet. It was the only difference they had ever had. When he had finally gone back to London, he had promised to return the following spring, if he could. But Easter had come and gone and no sign of him, and then shortly before Whitsun, Aunt Jessie's ill-used weak heart had finally given way, ironically enough as she sat watching one of her beloved sunsets over the western sea.

It was Jeremy's parting words that Catriona had remembered in the bewilderment of grief, when she had realised that the house would have to be sold to pay off various creditors, as well as the mortgage which she did not feel capable of shouldering.

'Here's my address.' He gave her a folded piece of paper. 'Keep it safe. If you ever need me, that's where I'll be.'

They had kissed and she had clung to him, her face wet with tears, promising to wait for him. At first his letters had come often and hers returned as eagerly. Then the frequency began to falter, although he still talked of the time when they would be together always. Now, if she faced it, five months had gone by with no word. Catriona had salved her pride by telling herself that Jeremy was busy with his studies and that he had important exams coming up, which, as he'd said in an early letter, could make all the difference to their future together. It was this, and the address carefully treasured in her trinket box at home, that had decided Catriona on her next course of action, now that she was alone.

She looked up from her reverie and found Mrs McGregor watching her concernedly. She smiled back at her.

'It'll be all right,' she said. 'I know it will. I can't bear to stay here with Auntie—and the house—gone like that. And

8

I can't bear to see what the Mackintoshes are going to do with the place either. Besides, London will be an adventure, and Jeremy will be there.' She smiled again, more gaily. 'I'll send you a piece of wedding cake.'

'So I should hope—when you find a husband,' Mrs McGregor said a trifle caustically.

She confided her misgivings to her husband over supper that evening.

'But she's set on it,' she added, and sighed. 'London's a gey long way to go, just to have your heart broken. I doubt yon poor lassie knows what she's getting herself into.'

A week later, standing completely bewildered in the bustle of Euston, Catriona was wondering exactly the same thing. The noise from the loudspeakers, the roar of the traffic outside, and the shouting and banging on the station itself as trains arrived and departed filled her with unreasoning panic. After the silence of Torvaig, where the hum of the telegraph wires was often clearly audible even in the middle of the day, she felt as if her eardrums would burst. What was worse, everyone but her seemed to know exactly where they were going. She followed the crowd to the barrier and gave up her ticket.

Outside in the sunlight, she felt even more uncomfortable. Jeremy's address was tucked safely in an inside pocket of her leather shoulder bag, but she had no idea how to get there. Awkwardly she shifted her rucksack on to her other shoulder and leaned her guitar case against a newsvendor's stand while she tried to take stock of her surroundings. Most of the money she possessed in the world—just under two hundred pounds—was safely locked up in a small cashbox in her rucksack, but she had kept a few pounds in her handbag for emergencies. Catriona decided ruefully that the first emergency was now. Picking up her guitar, she walked purposefully to the queue of people waiting for taxis. But when her turn came, she found to her astonishment that she

9

was calmly elbowed out of the way by two smartly dressed men. She stood indignantly on the pavement watching the last cab draw away, and a certain grimness crept into her expression. As another cab pulled up, a fur-coated woman stepped forward, brushing Catriona aside. Catriona swung her rucksack and there was a startled yelp as its bulk encountered the fur coat. The woman tottered, momentarily off balance, and Catriona squeezed past. 'Mine, I think,' she said, pushing her guitar case on to the back seat. She sat back feeling a little guilty at her discourtesy, but at the same time faintly victorious. If this was how Londoners conducted themselves, then a Muir could do just as well!

'Where to, ducks?'

'Oh.' Catriona produced Jeremy's slip of paper and pushed it through the glass partition. The driver looked at it and whistled. 'It's quite a way.' He turned and studied his passenger, from the attractive mass of curly dark hair on her shoulders down over the duffel coat and slim-fitting levis to the well-worn brogues. 'It'll cost you.'

'I have money.' Catriona lifted her chin at him.

'Suit yourself, love,' and he let in the clutch.

By the time the journey was over, Catriona was too sick with nervousness to worry over-much about the amount on the meter, although one corner of her thrifty soul registered a momentary squeal of outrage as she handed over the fare and added a generous tip.

'Shall I hang on?' asked the driver, apparently moved by the unexpected gesture.

Catriona looked up at the house where the cab had halted. It was not quite what she had envisaged, being a narrow terraced building with peeling stucco. The paintwork needed renewal, and the front garden was untended. Almost unconsciously Catriona's nose wrinkled. It was not the rendezvous she would have chosen for an ecstatic reunion with Jeremy. She bit her lip uncertainly. She wished now she had written to him in advance telling him that she was coming. She acknowledged now, standing in the dirty street, that she had been secretly afraid that he might try to deter her. For a moment she found it hard to remember even what Jeremy looked like, and again that odd sense of panic gripped her. She turned to the driver hesitantly.

'Perhaps—you would wait.'

She mounted the short flight of cracked steps and rang the bell.

'Probably not working, love,' the driver called. 'Bang on the door instead.'

Catriona complied with his advice, and after an endless moment or two the door was flung open. She was confronted by a thin woman in a soiled blue nylon overall, her hair in rollers under a yellow chiffon scarf.

'No vacancies,' she snapped, and made to close the door again.

Catriona stepped forward with a determination that she was far from feeling.

'I'm looking for one of your tenants, a Mr Jeremy Lord.'

'Are you now?' The woman's eyes appraised Catriona suggestively, lingering for a moment at her waistline. 'Well, you're too late, dear. He's gone.'

'Gone? Where?' Catriona felt the world spin round her. This was one development she had failed to take into account in her planning. Jeremy had told her she would find him here and she had believed him. She fought to remain calm.

'He left about three months ago. A nice Indian gentleman's got the room now.' The woman waited for a minute. 'Well, if that's all, dear, I must get on.'

Catriona moved impulsively. 'Did he—was there any forwarding address?'

'Now let me think. Some do, and some don't, of course. And there's a few who don't want to be traced.' She gave Catriona a malicious smile. 'But I'm sure that won't be true in your case, ducks. You wait here, while I see.' She disappeared to the rear of the musty hall and went through a door.

Catriona, fighting her tears, stood forlornly on the step. What if there was no address? She supposed there would be a hostel somewhere she could go to for the time being. Perhaps the driver would know. He seemed kind. Yet at the back of her mind were all the warnings she had ever heard about trusting strangers in big cities. She had never felt more alone, even at Aunt Jessie's funeral, for there the unspoken sympathy of the rest of the village had been like a rock for her to lean on. Here there was no one and nothing if Jeremy could not be found.

'Here we are, lovey.' The woman was coming back, flourishing a piece of paper. 'Mr Lord—11 Belmont Gardens. I thought I could recollect him saying where he was moving to.'

'Oh, thank you.' Catriona took the paper, realising that the woman's hand was remaining outstretched. For a moment she wondered if she was expected to shake hands, then she realised. Flushing, she dug into her shoulder bag and produced a pound note. Before she could say anything, it was gone from her hand and tucked away into a pocket of the nylon overall.

'That's very good of you, dear, very good.' The woman beamed at her. 'Now, if you were wanting a room, my first floor front is giving notice this week.'

'No,' Catriona said quietly. 'No, thanks. I must be going now.' And she ran back down the steps to the waiting taxi. She gave the new address to the driver.

'It's from the sublime to the gorblimey with you, girl,' he commented, as the cab drew away. 'Dead posh, Belmont Gardens.'

Catriona didn't find this piece of information particularly encouraging either. She realised for the first time how little she really knew about Jeremy and his background. She knew that he was an only child, and that both his parents were living, but little more.

It had never occurred to her during those happy sun-soaked days in Scotland to probe too deeply. Nor had she speculated too much while they were apart. She had preferred to remember the warmth of his kisses, and the glow in his eyes when he looked at her in that secret way that seemed to shut them off from the rest of the world even when others were there. These things were somehow more real than Jeremy's family, Jeremy's friends and the rest of his life in London in which as yet she had no part.

She realised of course that she would have to accept her part in them, but Jeremy had fitted so easily into her background that she had few doubts that she would slot as quickly into his. Now she was not so sure.

Looking out of the cab window, she realised the area they were in now was a marked improvement on the one where Jeremy used to live. Here the rows of houses were tall and spacious and trees edged the streets in neat lines.

The taxi turned right, swerving into a small square. In the centre of the square was a tiny railed-off park, with lawns, seats and flower beds. The houses that surrounded it were tall and elegant with delicately wrought iron railings in front of them. Many of them had window boxes filled with gay flowers, and Catriona could not help a little cry of pleasure and surprise.

'Told you so,' the driver commented smugly. He drew up with a flourish. 'Here we are, ducks—number eleven. Shall I bring your gear up?'

'I—I can manage, thank you.' Catriona was feeling nervous again. As the taxi drew away and vanished round the corner, she felt almost as if she just lost a friend. Her palms felt moist and she wiped them down the sides of her jeans, before shouldering her rucksack and picking up the guitar case.

'Here we go,' she thought, gazing up at the white façade of the house. A scarlet front door confronted her and as she counted the six immaculate steps which led to it, she noticed a gleaming brass bell surmounted by a name-plate in the wall.

The stark black lettering on the card seemed to leap out at her. 'J. Lord,' she read with relief, and pressed the bell.

Almost immediately she heard steps inside the house, and her stomach muscles contracted. She licked her dry lips, controlling her instinct to run away as quickly as she could, now that the moment of truth was here.

But it was a small woman, neatly dressed in a dark frock and apron, who opened the door this time, and looked at her inquiringly.

Catriona tried to speak with an assurance she was far from feeling.

'Mr Lord, please.'

'Well, I don't know, I'm sure, miss.' The woman looked at her searchingly, taking in the shabby coat and the ruck-sack. 'Is he expecting you?'

'Yes,' said Catriona, mentally crossing her fingers. It wasn't really a fib, she told herself. Jeremy had said she could come at any time. 'Please tell him Miss Muir is here.'

The woman held the door open and stood back to allow Catriona to enter. 'Come in, Miss Muir. I'll tell Mr Lord. Perhaps you'd like to leave your luggage in the hall.'

Catriona felt almost embarrassed to do so. It was a spacious hall with a black and white tiled floor and gleaming white walls. A carved chest stood against one wall support-ing a tall Chinese vase. She put her rucksack and guitar in a corner, where she hoped they would not be noticed, and followed the woman to a door on the right.

'Will you wait here, miss?' the woman asked, and Catriona nodded speechlessly. She had never seen such a room. The walls were covered in a heavy cream paper and

14

this colour was repeated in the thick fitted carpet. The floor-length curtains and luxurious suite were in a matching fabric which combined shades of sapphire and jade, and Catriona, who had always been told by Aunt Jessie, 'Blue and green should never be seen,' gasped at the effect this produced. The few other pieces of furniture—some occasional tables and a rosewood cabinet—were obviously antique and a cream marble mantelpiece bore a collection of exquisite Chinese porcelain dogs.

Catriona began to feel bewildered. What had Jeremy to do with all this luxury? She had never thought that he might be rich, but what other explanation was there for a life-style which was beyond anything she could have imagined? The shabby chintzes of Muir House had never seemed so far away.

Desperately she stared around. Oh, why had she come? What a fool she had been! There was no place for her here. The contrast between her own near-pennilessness and her present surroundings was a humiliation. And worst of all, one of her shoes had left a dirty mark on the carpet.

Tears sprang to her eyes, and she hurried towards the door, but almost simultaneously it was flung open, and Catriona halted with a gasp.

Regarding her was a tall man. He was wearing a dark silk dressing gown, and a towel was flung carelessly over one shoulder. His feet and legs were bare and one lock of damp-looking black hair hung down across his forehead. He put up a hand and brushed it impatiently away from the coldest grey eyes that Catriona had ever seen.

'Who are you?' she asked shakily. It was too much! The long journey, the lack of sleep, the first disappointment, and now this utter stranger looking her over as if she were an unprepossessing remnant on a bargain counter.

'That's rich, coming from you,' he commented, in a voice that matched his eyes. 'According to you, Miss—er—Muir, I'm expecting you.'

Catriona fought back the tears that were threatening to overwhelm her completely.

'Not you—Jeremy,' she said dolefully.

'Jeremy?' He gave her a long look, then closed the door behind him. 'I suppose I should have known. And what brings you here?'

Catriona stared at him helplessly. 'Doesn't—doesn't he live here?'

'No, by God, he doesn't,' was the forcible reply. 'What gave you that idea? Did he? I'll break his damned neck if . . .'

'No—oh, no. It was his landlady—his ex-landlady, that is. She said he'd left this as a forwarding address. And when I saw his name on the card at the door, I assumed . . .' Her voice tailed away uncomfortably as he looked her over with a certain grimness.

'Not his name, young woman. Mine. And this is my flat, and down the hall is my bedroom where I now propose to return now that this little misunderstanding has been cleared up. I did agree that Jeremy could have his mail sent on here for a short time, but that was over long ago.' He opened the door and held it, waiting for her to pass through. 'So if you'd be good enough to collect that weird clutter in the corner of the hall, we can go our separate ways.'

In spite of her distress, Catriona's temper began to rise. She had never been treated so summarily in her life before. Aunt Jessie wouldn't have behaved to a stray dog like this man was treating her, she thought furiously. Her first reaction was to do as he requested and stalk out of his house and his life without a backward glance. And yet he could obviously help her to find Jeremy, which at the moment seemed more important than salvaging her pride.

'I'm sorry to have intruded,' she began awkwardly. 'If you would just give me Jeremy's present address, I'll be happy to leave you in peace.'

'Out of the question,' he said abruptly. 'Good morning.'

'What do you mean?' Catriona faced him, openly indignant. 'Are you saying you won't tell me where he is?'

'Very perceptive,' he said smoothly, and Catriona longed to slap him hard across that dark sneering face. 'Now, on your way, my little orphan of the storm.'

'I'm not——' Catriona began to deny hotly, when it struck her with the suddenness of a blow that he was quite right. She was an orphan now. She looked at him mutely, unable to restrain her tears any longer.

'Oh, for God's sake,' he said bitingly. 'Do you think I haven't had that trick tried on me a hundred times? Only it's never worked in the past, and it's sure as hell not working now, darling.'

'I'm not your darling!' Catriona rubbed her eyes vigorously with a scrap of handkerchief she had found in her coat pocket. 'I think you're despicable!'

'No doubt you do. But just remember, you got yourself in here under false pretences, so don't start complaining when the going gets tough.' He gestured her towards the door.

'It wasn't false pretences,' Catriona protested. 'I asked for Mr Lord. I thought it would be Jeremy.'

'And instead it was me.' He pushed his hair back from his forehead again, almost wearily. 'A nasty shock for you, no doubt, and my advice to you is to go back where you came from as quickly as possible and get over it.'

'I can't go back,' Catriona said quietly. 'What's more, I came here to find Jeremy and I won't leave until I've seen him. And he'll not be very pleased when I tell him how you've treated me,' she added, a little vindictively.

But far from being perturbed, he merely smiled faintly.

'I don't think I have much to fear from that quarter,' he said. 'Tell me, why do you want to see him so urgently?'

'That's my business.' Catriona tilted her chin defiantly.

'On the contrary, you've also made it mine. Besides, his mother has been on at me for years to take a proper avuncular interest in the boy. Oh, I forgot,' he added satirically,

17

as Catriona's eyes flew startled to his face. 'I didn't introduce myself, did I. I'm Jason Lord, Jeremy's uncle.'

'I didn't know Jeremy had an uncle,' Catriona said numbly.

'Well, he didn't tell me about you either, so we're quits. Well, Miss Muir, I'm waiting.'

Catriona thrust her hands into the pockets of her coat to hide the fact that they were shaking. She met Jason Lord's scornful grey eyes with a flash of her green ones.

'In that case he probably hasn't told you either that we're in love and going to be married,' she said.

He had been lounging rather negligently against the door, but at that he stiffened instantly. His eyes went over her again, not with the same contempt as before, but assessing her, almost stripping her, while the colour rose in her cheeks.

'You're going to marry Jeremy,' he said slowly. 'What in hell's name gives you that idea?'

'He did. Last summer.'

'Which was a long time ago.' He looked at her wryly. 'And where was this—er—troth plighted, may I ask?'

'At Torvaig.' He still looked blank, so she explained, 'It's a little village on the west coast of Scotland. It's not very well known, but Jeremy found it while he was touring, and he stayed on.'

'I'll bet he did!' There was an almost savage note in the muttered words.

'Now will you let me see him?' she begged.

'No.' He spoke almost reflectively. 'In fact I think it's even more imperative that you use the other half of your return ticket and take yourself back to Torvaig and forget you ever knew Jeremy.'

'I'll do nothing of the sort!' she raged. 'I have a right to see him. I've come to London and I'm staying no matter what you say.'

'Look,' he came to stand in front of her and gripped her

18

arms tightly, his eyes bleak as a winter's day, 'I'm telling you for your own good. Forget him and go home. Can't you take my word for it that it's the best thing to do?'

'I wouldn't take your word for what day of the week it was,' Catriona said angrily, and his hands fell away from her so quickly that she swayed a little, feeling oddly dizzy.

'What's the matter?' he asked.

'I—I'm sorry. It's so warm in here.'

'Not that warm. Have you had anything to eat?'

'I had a few sandwiches on the train.' How long ago that seemed, she thought tiredly.

'That must have been a great comfort,' he said sarcastically. 'Well, you'd better take that appalling coat off and come with me.'

'To see Jeremy?' she asked hopefully.

'No,' he said witheringly. 'To have some breakfast before you pass out on me. I want you leaving here on your own two legs, not carried out on a stretcher.'

Catriona was just about to fling his insulting offer back in his face when it occurred to her how hungry she really was and how much better she would be able to continue the battle if she was fed. So more meekly than she felt, she allowed herself to be shepherded through the hall to the rear of the house and a large shiny kitchen.

It was a poem in gleaming ceramic tiles and stainless steel with gadgets Catriona had only ever seen before in magazine pictures. Remembering the old-fashioned sink and scrubbed wooden draining board back at Muir House, she felt a stab of envy. It seemed so unfair that Auntie Jessie had had to struggle with her work, while this unpleasant man had been living in the lap of luxury with hardly the need to lift a finger for himself.

'Mrs Birch!' he called, and the woman who had admitted Catriona came bustling in.

'Can you organise some breakfast for this starving morsel?' He indicated Catriona with a casual wave of his hand and she went hot with fury. 'Bacon and at least two eggs, I think. Oh, and porridge of course. She's from Scotland.'

'Porridge, sir?' Mrs Birch gaped at him. 'Well, I don't know if . . .'

'No,' Catriona interrupted hastily. 'I don't eat porridge.'

'Heresy,' Jason Lord said solemnly, but he was laughing at her, she knew. 'Well, grapefruit, then, and lots of coffee, Mrs B., and I'll have some as well.' He turned to Catriona. 'You'll be quite safe with Mrs Birch. I'm going to finish shaving and get dressed.'

Before Catriona could reply, he vanished.

Mrs Birch was setting out plates and cups and Catriona could already smell the bacon sizzling in the pan.

'Is there anything I can do?' she asked shyly.

'I can manage.' Mrs Birch gave her a quick glance. 'I should sit down before you fall down, lovey. You're as white as a sheet.'

Catriona complied shakily. 'I—I've had rather a shock.'

'Well, I wondered, though it's not for me to say. I could have told you he doesn't like seeing people so early in the morning. And when I saw that guitar I said to myself, Elsie, I said, she hasn't got a prayer, poor little soul.'

'My guitar?' Catriona echoed bewilderedly.

'He doesn't do musical acts, lovey. It's all current affairs and documentaries. I thought you'd have known that.'

And as Catriona continued to stare at her in amazement, she tutted impatiently.

'Well, you do know who he is, don't you?'

'All I know is that he's Jeremy's uncle,' Catriona admitted.

'Lord above!' Mrs Birch cracked the first of the eggs into the pan. 'He's a TV producer, dear. He does *Here and Now* on a Monday, apart from anything else. And his documentary on alcoholics last year got an award.'

'I'm afraid I've never seen much television,' Catriona

said quietly. 'We didn't have a set at home.'

Mrs Birch was obviously as staggered by this as if Catriona had suddenly grown a second head.

'Well, there's a thing,' she said at last. 'And there was me thinking you were pestering him for a job.'

Catriona coloured. 'Oh, it's nothing like that,' she said.

'I'm pleased to hear it.' Mrs Birch set half a grapefruit frosted with sugar in front of Catriona and lowered her voice confidentially. 'You see, dear, the better known he's become, the worse it's got. A lot of girls just think he's the key to fame and fortune and heaven knows what. He knows so many people in television, you see, and one word from him can do all sorts. I'm glad you're not one of them.' She beamed approvingly at Catriona, then turned back to the cooker. 'Now you get started, because this is nearly ready.'

Catriona had almost finished her eggs and bacon by the time Jason Lord returned. In a silk-textured dark suit he looked even more forbidding, she thought, and had to fight an urge to flinch as he slid on to the stool next to hers at the breakfast bar.

'That's better,' he remarked coolly. 'You're beginning to look more like a human being.'

Mrs Birch put two steaming cups of coffee down on the bar and hurried out of the kitchen to her other chores.

'You've placed me under an obligation to you——' Catriona began stiffly, but he interrupted.

'Then repay it—please—by going home.'

'I have no home.'

'You just thought you'd move in with my nephew.' His tone was glacial again.

'No,' she answered wretchedly. 'I've told you—we're going to be married.'

He glanced meaningly at her ringless hands. 'You're officially engaged?'

She hesitated miserably, unwilling to share even part of her precious secret with this man. Then, very slowly, she undid the top two buttons on her white shirt blouse and pulled out the silver chain she wore round her neck. There were two metal objects hanging on it—a small key and a silver ring set with a cairngorm. A cheap enough trinket, but Jeremy had bought it for her one day in Fort William.

'Until I can afford a proper one,' he had whispered as he put it on her finger and kissed her. She had thought she would die of happiness, and some of that remembered joy lingered in her face as she extended the ring to Jason Lord in the soft curve of her palm.

There was a long silence. Then, 'I see,' he said in a voice devoid of any emotion. She looked at him, puzzled, but his eyes were veiled as he looked down at the thin trail of smoke from the cigarette held lightly between his fingers.

'You will let me see him, won't you?' Her voice was pleading.

'Yes.' He stubbed the cigarette out with sudden violence. 'Yes, Miss Muir, you win. I'll take you to him this evening.'

'Not till this evening?' She couldn't believe her victory, but at the same time this apparently unnecessary delay jarred on her. 'Why not now?'

'Because he's away. He'll be back this evening—his mother's giving a party. I didn't intend to go, but now I will and I'll take you with me.'

'But I couldn't let you do that,' Catriona said at once. It was not at all how she had planned to see Jeremy again, at a party against a background where she would be an interloper. 'I'd be a gatecrasher. And besides, I haven't anything to wear.'

'The eternal cry of woman, but in your case it could just be true,' he said, his eyes flicking over her dismissively. 'And you won't be a gatecrasher. You'll go as my guest. Marion always expects me to bring a girl-friend to her parties.'

Catriona felt a quick surge of revulsion at the idea of being taken for his girl-friend.

22

'I'm sure there are other people you'd rather take,' she said awkwardly.

'Dozens,' he retorted. Suddenly he leaned forward and his long fingers brushed the small curve of her breast. Startled, she pulled away, feeling oddly as if she had been scorched by a sudden flame.

'Don't be a fool,' he said. 'Give me credit for a little more subtlety in my approach than that. I'm just curious to know what this is.'

It was the key that shared the chain with the ring.

'That's just the key of my cashbox,' she said a little nervously.

'Cashbox?' he queried, with raised brows. 'What cashbox?'

So perforce Catriona found herself telling him about Auntie Jessie and the sale of Muir House.

'So when all was settled I had about two hundred pounds altogether. I spent some of it of course on my ticket and on a taxi today. But the rest is in a box in my rucksack,' she added, noticing with alarm that he was frowning again.

'You've been carrying all the money you possess in the world around London with you all morning!' he said with ominous calm. 'And supposing you'd been robbed? Dear God, girl, you're not safe to be allowed out!'

'I can look after my money and myself,' Catriona said indignantly.

'Can you now?' he said softly. 'So much so that you blunder into a strange man's flat, make all kinds of demands and stay for breakfast without any thought of what you might have to give in return.'

'I'm quite willing to pay you——' she began, but he silenced her by placing an authoritative finger on her parted lips. An odd shiver ran through her. She had never been touched, she told herself, by anyone she loathed as much as him.

'But supposing I asked for payment in kind rather than

23

cash?' His eyes held hers and she was aware that her breathing had quickened involuntarily.

'I'd scream for Mrs Birch,' she found herself saying with amazing calmness.

'You assume she'd be on your side. Well, she probably would. She has a weakness for waifs and strays.' With an insouciance that infuriated her, he let the key and ring drop back inside the neck of her shirt. They felt disturbingly warm from his fingers and again she felt that unaccountable shiver.

'Well,' he slid off the stool, 'studio for me, and bed, I think, for you.'

'Bed?' Catriona gasped.

'Of course. Don't tell me you got much sleep on that train last night.'

'No—but I can't sleep here.'

'Why not?' he asked. 'And don't start behaving like an hysterical virgin. I've already told you, I'm going to work. I'll get Mrs Birch to wake you around two-thirty and I'll be back at three to take you shopping.'

'Shopping?'

'Must you repeat everything I say?' he said with studied patience.

'But I don't need to go shopping.' Catriona thought desperately of her small store of money. She could not go to Jeremy completely empty-handed.

'Oh yes, you do. You need a party dress,' he said coolly. Before she could argue, he was gone, and a moment later she heard the front door slam.

Catriona leant on the breakfast bar. Her head was throbbing, and she pressed her finger tips against her forehead with a little sigh. He was everything that was detestable, she thought, and he seemed to take a perverse delight in unnerving her. Only the thought that when evening came he would take her to Jeremy stopped her from grabbing up her things and running away as fast as she could.

24

'Come along, lovey.' Mrs Birch's voice was kind. 'A nice lie down is what you want. You'll feel better in no time.'

Catriona found herself in a small bedroom furnished in muted browns and yellows with a thick continental quilt on the single bed. It was incredibly soft and warm and she felt an almost sensuous relaxation as she stretched out under it.

'A good sleep,' Mrs Birch was saying somewhere a long way off. 'A good sleep.'

Catriona slept.

CHAPTER TWO

SHE was awoken by a hand on her shoulder. Mrs Birch in outdoor clothes was standing by the bed, holding a small tray.

'Coffee, miss,' she announced. 'Mr Lord will be back soon. I'd be ready if I were you. He hates being kept waiting.'

Catriona was sorely tempted to proclaim her total indifference to Mr Lord's likes and dislikes, but she knew that under the circumstances, that would be churlish.

'The bathroom's just across the hall, and I've put clean towels in there in case you want a shower,' Mrs Birch went on. 'Now if that's all, miss, I'll be getting along.'

'Thank you. You've been very kind,' Catriona said sincerely.

'It's been a pleasure,' Mrs Birch replied brightly. 'I hope we meet again, miss. And if I might say so'—she lowered her voice confidentially—'I wouldn't wear the jeans, miss. Not up West anyway. Fine for the Kings Road, but I don't suppose you'll be going there.' And she was gone.

Catriona finished her coffee and slid out of bed. The unpopular jeans and her shirt were lying on the dressing stool and she picked them up, her face a little mutinous. All she had in her rucksack were two cotton dresses she had made last week, and some woollen sweaters. Tossing her dark hair determinedly from her face, she marched off to find the bathroom.

She was brushing her hair back into a ponytail and securing it with an elastic band when Jason Lord returned. She heard him come whistling down the hall and pause outside her door, and she squared her shoulders.

'Are you ready, Miss Muir?' he called.

'Quite ready.' She picked up her duffel coat and walked to the door. Somewhat to her surprise, he gave her a mocking grin as she emerged into the hall.

'I like a girl who sticks to her principles,' he commented as his eyes ran over her. 'Come, Cinderella, you shall go to the ball.'

Her blood boiling, she followed him to the front door and down the steps to the sleek cream-coloured car that awaited them. Jason Lord held the door open for her and she subsided a little awkwardly into the low tan leather seat on the passenger side. She stared entranced at the dashboard, wondering what the various buttons and dials could be for.

'Do you drive?' He slid into the seat beside her, and flicked the ignition expertly. The car started immediately, and they pulled away.

'I had a few lessons, but I never took the test.'

'A pity. It's an advantage, wherever you happen to live,' he said.

'Perhaps Jeremy will teach me.'

'Perhaps he will,' he returned noncommittally.

Catriona tried to make note of each turn they took, but she was soon bewildered. The streets were wider now, and the traffic was getting heavy. The houses were giving way to shops too, and as they drove along Catriona saw signs advertising more theatres and restaurants than she had ever dreamed existed.

'I've never seen so many people,' she remarked impulsively, then regretted sounding so naïve.

'You should see it on Sundays. It's almost as quiet as Torvaig,' he said. 'And what's more, I've seen a vacant parking meter. Here we go.'

A few minutes later, Catriona found herself in a huge shop. Jason Lord's hand was under her elbow, urging her forward through the crowds thronging the counters, as she caught tantalising glimpses of exquisite displays of scarves and handbags and sniffed exotic odours as she was whisked through the cosmetics department.

'Lift or escalator?' he asked, then quickly, 'I'm sorry, I'm treating you like a child. But you look so damned young in those jeans with your hair tied back.'

'I know—like a waif,' she retorted, already more than conscious that she seemed to be the only person in jeans in the whole massive building. 'And I've never been on an escalator.'

'Up we go, then.' He steadied her on to the moving staircase. 'Hold on to me if you like.'

'The rail is quite adequate,' she returned stiffly, then spoiled it by stumbling as they stepped off at the top.

Her feet sank into a thick carpet, and somewhere soft music was playing. Everywhere there were clothes, displayed on models, pinned on wire frames, hanging on rails and circular racks. She felt she was dreaming, and then another more demoralising thought struck her. She caught at Jason Lord's sleeve.

'My money! I—I left it in the rucksack.'

'Well?' He looked tall and forbidding as he swung to look at her. 'What of it?'

Catriona gestured awkwardly around her.

'I haven't enough with me to pay for anything here.'

'I never suggested you should. Now come on. We've a lot

to get through.' He sounded impatient. 'First things first. We don't even know whether you'll find a dress you like here.'

'But they must have hundreds of dresses,' Catriona gasped.

'You're an unusual woman if that makes any difference,' he said. 'Ah, there's the person we want.' He propelled Catriona towards a grey-haired woman in a smart black suit, standing by a rail of coats studying some papers. 'Hello, Mrs Cuthbert. We need your help.'

'Mr Lord.' The woman smiled charmingly, then turned to Catriona. 'My word!' she said.

'And that's putting it mildly.' Jason Lord took Catriona by the shoulders and pushed her forward. 'She's going to Mrs Lord's party with me and she hasn't a thing to wear. What can you do for her?'

Mrs Cuthbert studied Catriona, now flushed with humiliation.

'Well, there are possibilities,' she said cautiously. 'What does she need?'

'The works.' Jason Lord released Catriona and stepped back. 'And her hair, Mrs Cuthbert. I don't know who attends to my sister-in-law, but . . .'

'It's Miss Barbara,' said Mrs Cuthbert. 'I'll phone the salon now and see if she can squeeze another appointment in.'

'Fine.' He consulted his watch. 'Shall we say the restaurant in two hours?'

'I'll send her to you,' Mrs Cuthbert promised.

Catriona raged inwardly. They might have been talking about one of the dummy figures standing round the department, she thought furiously. And just who was going to pay for all this? She still had to find somewhere to live until she and Jeremy could be married. She could not afford to spend any of her little hoard of money on a party dress she did not need. But Jason Lord's tall figure was already disappearing, and Mrs Cuthbert was leading her gently but firmly to a fitting room.

Later that evening, Catriona stood in front of the mirror in the small bedroom at the flat and looked at herself in frank disbelief.

The dress was almost the same green as her eyes, and its low bodice cut square across her small breasts was covered with sparkling crystals with narrow matching shoulder-straps. The straight satin skirt reached the floor, hiding her delicately strapped high-heeled sandals.

She was really Cinderella, she thought wonderingly.

Her hair, expertly trimmed, had been set so that it hung smooth and shining to her shoulders, just turning up at the ends. She was lightly made up, with eye-shadow and mascara used just as the girl in the beauty salon had shown her, and her lips glowed a pale rose. A small evening bag, studded with crystals, lay on the dressing table. She picked it up, and putting the long stole that matched the dress over her arm, went down the hall to the room where she had met Jason Lord.

He was standing leaning on the mantelpiece, with a glass in his hand. He looked up as she entered, and she paused nervously waiting for some barbed remark. But the silence stretched on endlessly, and she felt oddly disappointed.

'Would you like a drink?' There was a formal note in his voice.

'No—thank you.'

'Right.' He finished what was left in his glass and put it down. 'We'll be off, then.' He took the stole from her and placed it round her shoulders. She was acutely aware of his touch on her bare skin and moved away restively.

They drove for a long time in silence. Catriona kept stealing looks at her companion, but his eyes were firmly fixed on the road and all she saw was his hard profile. He too had a chin, she noticed, and a nasty habit of expecting his own way to match it. Which reminded her of the worry that had been nagging her all afternoon even through her bewildered enjoyment of choosing the dress, and its underwear and accessories, and the hair-do and beauty treatment that followed.

'This dress is outrageous,' she informed him.

'I wouldn't say so.' He still did not look at her. 'A little more revealing than you're probably used to, that's all.'

'I didn't mean that, and you know it,' said Catriona hotly. 'I mean the price.'

'Don't worry about it,' he told her lightly. 'After all, it's in the family, isn't it? And Jeremy's mother has an account there, as you may have gathered. We could charge it to her, if you'd rather.'

'We'll do no such thing——' Catriona began, then saw his lips twitch. 'You're laughing at me again,' she said uncertainly.

'A little,' he said. 'Why not forget about the cost of it all, and start thinking about what you're going to say to Jeremy. Surely that's more important than anything else. Concentrate on the dialogue, darling, and forget the props. They're just incidental.'

'I wish you wouldn't call me darling!'

'I know you do.' He sent her a swift glance, one mocking brow raised. 'And so—darling—I do it all the more.'

'Just to annoy me?'

'You do rise to the bait so beautifully—and so regularly,' he said.

Catriona lifted her chin and stared through the windscreen into the darkness. Jeremy's parents, she had learned, lived just outside Staines near the river. She supposed that one day she would be familiar with this route, and with the house they were bound for. Now she felt totally at sea, and it frightened her to realise that she was wholly dependent on this stranger beside her. After all, she only had his word for

30

it that there was a party at all. He could be taking her any-where.

The car slowed steadily, then turned through a pair of white gates and up a shallow drive.

Catriona saw the lights of a large house and heard the steady beat of music close at hand. There were a lot of other cars parked in the drive and on the gravelled sweep in front of the house, and she sat quietly as Jason manoeuvred his vehicle into one of the remaining spaces.

When he opened the door for her, she sat still for a moment, marshalling her courage.

'Cold feet?' he inquired.

'I'm perfectly warm, thanks,' she returned, deliberately misunderstanding him. His hand closed round hers as he helped her out of the car, and for a moment she almost returned the pressure of his fingers. But just in time she remembered who he was, and the treatment she had been forced to put up with from him, and snatched her hand away.

'Come along then, Miss Muir,' he said, and she was startled to hear the harsh note back in his voice. 'This is what you wanted. Make the most of it.'

Inside the house, Catriona was startled to find a uni-formed maid waiting to take their coats.

'Don't worry,' Jason murmured. 'She's not permanent staff. Just hired for the big occasion.'

He guided her expertly through groups of chatting people in the hall into a large room with a bar at one end. Catriona noticed that French windows stood open at one side, lead-ing apparently to a big conservatory.

'There's Clive—never far from the drinks,' he remarked. 'Brace yourself, darling, you're about to meet my respected brother, and Jeremy's papa.'

Clive Lord was shorter than his brother with slightly receding hair and a developing paunch. He looked much older than Jason too, but in his smile Catriona thought she could detect a reminder of Jeremy, and she warmed to him.

'I don't think I've seen you here with Jason before, have I, Miss—er—Muir?' he asked, handing her a glass filled with a glowing red liquid.

'Please call me Catriona,' she said, smiling up at him, and ignoring Jason's sardonic smile.

'I don't suppose you know how honoured you are, Clive,' he murmured. 'When's the big moment, by the way?'

'Oh—shortly.' Clive looked round in a harassed manner. 'I don't see the need for all this fuss. We had the same nonsense in Yorkshire last week. But you know Marion—not to be outdone, of course.'

'Of course,' Jason agreed smoothly. 'Come on, my sweet, we don't want to miss anything.'

Catriona felt her temper rising. 'What's going on?' she asked heatedly. 'Where's Jeremy? I must see him alone for a few moments.'

'We're going to see him now. I should put that revolting concoction Clive gave you down if I were you. There'll be champagne in the next room.'

'I don't want any champagne,' Catriona insisted almost wildly.

'Oh, but you must. It's traditional, and the fun's just beginning.' He drew her across the hall into a room packed with people. It was quite true—there was champagne, and Catriona took the glass she was offered almost mechanically.

'That's the ticket.' Clive appeared beside them beaming. 'Now I must do my stuff, I suppose.' He went off through the crowd, and just as Catriona was turning to Jason, a demand to be taken to Jeremy at once framing on her lips, a sudden hush fell.

Startled, she looked round, and then—at last—she saw Jeremy. He was standing at the end of the room with two women. One of them, Catriona was immediately convinced, was his mother. She was tall and fair-haired, wearing an expensive dress, and stood toying nervously with her rings.

32

Although she was smiling, Catriona had the feeling that in repose Mrs Lord's face would have a rather peevish expression, and she felt slightly chilled. At the same time she was registering incredulously that the other woman—hardly more than a girl, in fact—was clinging possessively to Jeremy's arm. He was in evening dress, and he had shaved off his beard and cut his hair. He looked quite different, Catriona thought with dismay, then he turned to the pretty, rather plump blonde at his side, smiling at something she had said, and his smile made him the familiar reassuring Jeremy again.

Clive's voice rang out over the room.

'And now, everyone—friends—if you'll raise your glasses, we'll drink a toast to Jeremy and Helen. Long life and every happiness!'

Catriona stood numbly, her fingers clenched round the slender stem of the glass as Jeremy bent and kissed the girl, who smiled and held up her left hand so that everyone could see the glittering diamond ring adorning it.

Catriona gave a little choking cry. The room dipped and blurred and she heard her glass smash to the parquet floor as she turned and fled. A startled maid stepped forward, as she gained the hall.

'Excuse me, madam——' she began as Catriona began blindly to wrestle with the ornate ring that served as a front door handle. Her hands were slippery with perspiration, and she felt hysteria rising within her. Then Jason's hands were gripping her shoulders, and his voice was saying calmly, 'Come into the conservatory, darling. It's cooler there, and you won't catch a chill as you might outside.'

His grip was inexorable. It was like trying to tear free from a vice, and Catriona did not have the strength to struggle any more. She allowed him to lead her across the room they had first entered to the French windows. He lifted one of the long beige velvet curtains, and she passed through like an automaton.

Ordinarily Catriona would have delighted in the warm exotic scents and sights around her. Hanging lamps had been festooned across the glass roof, and the lights were reflected back from the banks of glossy leaves and petals and from a tiny sunken pool. Small brightly coloured fish darted among the pebbles and the lilies, and Catriona stood watching them, her mind registering with complete detachment every swift movement and ripple of the water. In spite of the more than mild atmosphere, she felt icy cold.

'Here.' Jason appeared, holding a glass which he thrust into her hand. 'Drink this, and don't drop it this time. Caterers' glasses are an expensive item, as you being a thrifty Scot should know.'

Obediently she swallowed some of the amber liquid, then choked as the powerful spirit caught her throat. It was a violent revival, but it was what she needed, and it gave her the courage to face him.

'You knew,' she accused, her voice almost breaking. 'You knew!'

'Of course I did.' He set one foot on the low parapet of the pool, and took a brief sip from his own glass.

'And you didn't tell me?'

'No.'

'How could you be so cruel?' she whispered, her eyes and throat smarting with the tears she wouldn't allow to fall.

'I had to be cruel—to be kind,' he said. His dark face was angry as he stared at her. 'I did my level best to scare you off, to get rid of you, even. I told you to go back to Scotland, but no. Nothing gainsays Miss Catriona Muir once her mind is made up, does it?'

'Why didn't you tell me the truth?' she asked, trying to control her trembling voice.

He looked at her steadily. 'Because nothing on God's earth would have convinced you that it was the truth. You had Jeremy cast as the hero, and me, most definitely, as the villain of the piece. Any warning I had given you about

Helen's existence you would have dismissed as having an ulterior motive, though God knows what makes you think I harbour any towards you,' he added.

She stood silent for a moment, torn between the justice of what he had said and the misery that was threatening to engulf her.

'Here,' he said quietly, as if he sensed her struggle, and passed her the white handkerchief from his breast pocket. This unexpected consideration was the final straw. She sank down on to a wicker lounger and let her tears have full rein at last.

To her relief, he made no attempt to touch her, apart from taking the remains of the brandy from her. Except for the sudden flare of his lighter as he lit a cigarette, she was hardly aware of his presence.

Eventually, as her self-control returned and the tearing sobs began to subside, she sat up slowly, dreading that he would be watching her, mocking her woebegone appearance, but he was merely sitting by the side of the pool, staring down at the immaculate toe of one of his black shoes.

She forced herself to sound calm. 'Who is she, please?'

He glanced up. 'Helen? Oh, the original poor little rich girl. Her father's in wool—the family live near Bradford. She met Jeremy in Kitzbuhl a couple of years ago.'

'If he's known her all that time, how could he have been the way he was with me?' she said slowly.

He shrugged. 'As you may have gathered, I've never had much time for Jeremy. He was damnably spoiled when he was a child. I don't think Clive ever realised how much until it was too late. Marion's a bit of a fool, and I've never thought her feelings go particularly deep, so maybe Jeremy takes after her.'

'Just like that,' she said unsteadily.

'What do you want me to say?' he countered, harshly. 'It's all been a terrible mistake, and it's you he really loves? And all you have to do is go back in that room looking like the Queen of Elfland and he'll be yours for ever more?'

'He did love me,' Catriona whispered, her lips trembling. 'He did. I know it.'

'I daresay he did in his way for a while—if that's any consolation. But I can promise you this, even if he did love you as you believed, he still wouldn't give up Helen's money for you. And Marion wouldn't let him either.'

'You devil,' she said very distinctly.

He gave a slight laugh. 'Poor Cinderella! All the way to the ball to find Prince Charming's turned into a pumpkin, and you have to go home with Bluebeard.'

Catriona stared down at the handkerchief she was still holding. It had his initials in the corner, she noticed, and she recalled that Jeremy's had been the same. Her eyes began to prick again.

'Oh no,' Jason Lord said decisively, and stood up. 'I've had enough of that, Miss Muir. You've probably raised the humidity in here already and killed off Marion's prize specimens. Now we're going to do some straight talking.'

'What is there to say?' she said hopelessly. 'I just can't understand why you brought me here—like this.' She touched the shimmering length of her skirt with distaste.

'Then you're even less perceptive than I gave you credit for,' he said coldly. 'That charming piece of nonsense you're wearing is a disguise. Do you think anyone here tonight gave you a second glance except as an extremely attractive young woman? If I'd just given you the address and allowed you simply to turn up in those damned jeans and that rucksack, it would have made a nine days' wonder for all of them in there. Is that what you wanted? Everyone staring at you, and laughing—because they would have laughed, make no mistake about that, my child. Okay, so you've been humiliated, but no one knows that except the two of us. Oh—and Jeremy, I think,' he added sarcastically as she turned startled eyes towards him. 'I think he caught your misguided exit just now. He looked as if he'd just been pole-

36

axed anyway. But to everyone else, you're just Jason's new girl, whether you like it or not.'

'I must leave,' she said.

'Presently. We still have things to discuss.'

'I have nothing to discuss with you, Mr Lord,' she said quietly.

He threw down his cigarette, stubbing it out with his shoe.

'All right,' he said. 'You're hurt and you're angry because I've brought you down from Cloud Seven with a jolt. But you'd have been forced down eventually, Catriona, don't you see that? You came to London of your own free will, and you saw Jeremy as you insisted on doing. Now it's time to pick up the pieces. You weren't just crying for Jeremy just now, you know. You were crying for first love and all it means. Well, first love isn't everything.'

'Oh, I believe you,' she said with bitter sarcasm. 'I'm sure you're an expert. It must run in the family.'

'You little bitch,' he said slowly. 'But even if you were right, at least I conduct my affairs with women who know what the score is. I don't take sweets from babies. Only a child could have been taken in by someone as callow as Jeremy.'

'I suppose I deserved that,' she said wearily. She held out her hand. 'Goodbye, Mr Lord. It's been salutory, if nothing else.'

He ignored the gesture. 'How do you intend to leave here, and where do you propose to go?'

Catriona was taken aback. 'There are taxis, I suppose. And hotels.'

'There are,' he agreed. 'But only if you have money. And some of the more respectable hotels also like you to have luggage.'

Catriona was silent. It was like playing chess with an expert, she thought. Every move she tried to make was anticipated and blocked.

'So let's look at the alternative,' he went on calmly. 'Go

upstairs and repair your make-up and have the inevitable confrontation with Jeremy. Oh yes,' he took her chin in his hand as she flinched involuntarily, 'you can tell him what tale you like, as long as it's not the unvarnished truth. Don't let him have that satisfaction. And then I'll take you home, pride intact.'

It did not occur to Catriona until she was sitting in one of the elaborately furnished bedrooms, renewing her lipstick, that Jason Lord had not specified precisely where 'home' was.

As he had predicted, it was inevitable when she emerged from the bedroom that Jeremy was waiting outside.

'Trina!' His face was white, and he moistened his lips nervously. 'I couldn't believe it. What on earth are you doing here? Who brought you?'

Afterwards Catriona was amazed at the way the lie sprang so readily to her lips.

'Oh, I know it was mean,' she said, smiling radiantly at him. 'But Jason and I just thought what a joke it would be if I—turned up, like a skeleton from the past. And your face was marvellous when you saw me. I wouldn't have missed it.'

Relief was struggling with incredulity on his face. 'You're Jason's girl?' he queried sharply.

'Quite correct.' Jason himself joined them, looking faintly amused. 'I don't think you realise just what you've let slip through your fingers this time, dear nephew.'

Jeremy laughed uneasily. 'Oh, Trina's an angel. I—I don't blame you at all. It was just such a—surprise.'

'Well, the world's full of surprises,' Catriona said gaily. 'Poor lamb, I should have let you know I was here, but Jason has hardly given me time to breathe since I got to London.'

Jason came to stand beside her, dropping his arm lightly across her shoulders. She felt the usual urge to draw away, but was forced to stand still in his embrace, trapped by her

38

own pretence. She noticed he was carrying her stole over his arm.

'Are you leaving already?' Jeremy asked, his voice sharp with curiosity.

'Why, yes.' Before Catriona could move, or protest, Jason bent and kissed her slowly and deliberately on the mouth. 'It's time, I think, that all good little girls were in bed,' he went on, smiling down into her outraged eyes.

Jeremy flushed, and he looked at Catriona with unmistakable speculation.

'So that's how it is. Fine. Be happy,' he said, with a fair attempt at nonchalance.

'Besides,' there was no disguising the amusement in Jason's voice, 'Sally would never forgive me if I kept Catriona out too late.'

Jeremy looked at him quickly. 'Sally Fenton? Is Trina staying with her? I—see.'

'I doubt it,' Jason said lightly, and took Catriona's hand. 'Come on, love, time to go. Tell your mother I'll phone her,' he added to the nonplussed Jeremy as he led Catriona away.

In the car she turned on him furiously. 'How dared you?'

'How dared I do what?' He was infuriatingly unruffled as the car moved down the drive and nosed out on to the road.

'Paw me in that insulting way!' she raged, and was further incensed by his laughter.

'You flatter yourself, Miss Muir.' He flashed her a swift glance. 'Surely that can't have been the most strenuous embrace you've experienced. I must have a word with Jeremy.'

'Oh, shut up,' she said bitterly. 'At least with Jeremy I never felt—besmirched.'

Something came and went in his face, but his voice was still amused. 'I'm sure you would have done—in time.'

She sought for a retort that would silence him once and for all, but none was forthcoming, so she retired behind a hostile tight-lipped barrier of silence.

Jason Lord seemed totally unconcerned. He hummed snatches of tunes, commented on the road conditions and eventually with a courteous, 'I hope you don't mind,' switched on the radio. It was a foreign station. Catriona could not recognise the announcer's accent, but the music they were playing had an oddly soothing quality. The street lights and the white lines on the road became fused in a soft blurring of consciousness. Her head slipped sideways on to her companion's shoulder, and her breathing became soft and even.

She was floating on a cloud, weightless and carefree. Jeremy was beside her, his kisses light as Highland mist on her face. How warm she was, how safe. Then a shadow came between them, and someone was shaking the cloud, which was breaking up and dissolving. It was Jason Lord, his face satyr-like. 'Come down off Cloud Seven, Miss Muir,' he was saying. 'Come down. Come down.' And his hands were hard on her shoulders, shaking her so that she tried to cry out, only the cloud was muffling her.

Gasping for breath, she struggled out from under the Continental quilt to find Jason Lord standing over her with a cup and saucer.

'You are a violent little thing in the mornings,' he commented sarcastically. 'Do you want this coffee in bed or over it?'

Catriona stared at him for one panic-stricken moment, then huddled the quilt over her bare shoulders.

'It's all right,' he said with studied patience. 'It's only your dress that's missing. I assumed you wouldn't want to ruin it by sleeping in it, so I put it on a hanger in the wardrobe.'

'You did—what?'

'Oh, grow up,' he snapped. 'You surely don't think there's anything indecent in that boned effort and long waist slip

40

you're wearing. There were women at the party last night showing twice as much.'

Catriona was crimson from head to foot. 'Do you mind telling me what I'm doing here?' she inquired icily.

'With pleasure.' He sat down on the edge of the bed, to her immediate alarm. 'You're here as a very temporary lodger, and as soon as I can get Sally Fenton on the telephone and talk her into taking you on, you're leaving.'

Catriona quivered. 'I don't know that I care to be passed on like an unwanted package,' she began.

'And I don't know that you have any choice,' he interrupted. 'I happen to know Sally is looking for another girl to share with, and it could be a way out of the woods for us both. I'm not happy at the idea of you drifting out into the city jungle with no one to keep an eye on you.'

'I'm not a child,' Catriona said defiantly.

'Oh, no. Your actions have been characterised by your maturity since you got off the train,' he retorted.

'But I don't know this Sally,' she protested.

'You know her as well as most girls who share flats these days. Often they just answer each other's ads. In your case, it's me doing the arranging instead of a newspaper. And I'm sure you'll like Sally.'

'Well, that makes everything all right, doesn't it?' she said, trying to emulate his sarcasm.

'Only you can do that,' he told her. 'You say you have nowhere to return to in Scotland. You may as well live up to the story you told nephew Jeremy and try enjoying yourself in London for a change. Sally'll help you find a job of some kind. She's an actress, so she's used to finding herself temporary work between engagements.'

'I see.' Catriona stared unseeingly at the pattern on the quilt. 'All right, I'll give it a try. And—thank you,' she added with difficulty.

'Well, let's not strain common civility any further,' he

41

said, but he was smiling. 'Come on, drink this while it's still hot.'

Catriona accepted the cup meekly and began to sip. She allowed Jason Lord to reach the door before halting him with a wide-eyed, 'Oh, Mr Lord. Forgive me for asking, but is Sally—one of your women?'

She expected an angry outburst, but instead he leaned against the door, smiling lazily.

'No, as a matter of fact, though I'm flattered by your interest,' he said. 'Can it be because you imagine you've joined those select ranks yourself?'

In spite of the sheltering quilt and her quite adequate covering beneath it, Catriona felt naked under his insolent gaze.

'If so, let me disabuse your little head of any such notion.' His voice lengthened to a drawl. 'As I told you last night, I don't take sweets from babies, especially when they're asleep. Among other things I require of "my women", as you so elegantly put it, is that they at least remain awake and give me their undivided attention. You fail on both counts.'

And the door closed behind him, as the pillow, hurled with all the force Catriona could muster, thudded against it.

Almost in spite of herself, Catriona found that she liked Sally Fenton on sight. Sally was small and red-headed with delicate mobile features and an impish smile. Her eyes were dancing as she flung open the front door of the flat.

'Jason, angel!' She flung herself rapturously at him. 'You've saved my life. Ever since that idiot Jill went back to Birmingham, I've been desperate.'

'Careful, Sal.' Jason disengaged himself and sent a glinting look at Catriona. 'You'll be giving Miss Muir the wrong idea.'

'Miss Muir? Oh, surely not. It's Catriona, isn't it, just like in Robert Louis Stevenson,' Sally said gaily, taking her hands. 'Please come in and say you like it and that you'll stay for at least a little while. I need the extra rent—not to mention the company.'

'Don't tell her that,' Jason admonished, sitting on the edge of the table and lighting a cigarette. 'She's a Scot and intensely money-conscious.'

'That's not true,' Catriona began indignantly, then subsided as Sally exclaimed, 'Oh, just ignore him. He says the most appalling things about everyone. But we have to forgive him because he's so important—aren't you, darling?' And she wrinkled her nose at him.

'Not important to you, at any rate, Sally,' he said drily. 'I'll fetch Miss Muir's things from the car.'

'And we'll make up the other bed,' Sally said. 'The bedroom's only tiny, I'm afraid. I hope you haven't got too many clothes.'

Catriona swallowed. 'I've hardly got any,' she admitted.

'Oh.' Sally swung round and regarded her for a moment. 'Well, that's super. We can go shopping. Don't look so frightened—you don't have to spend the earth to create a good effect. And it will be no good applying to the agency I go to in jeans,' she added practically. 'A trouser suit, perhaps, but those have rather seen better days, haven't they?'

It was impossible to take offence, Catriona thought amusedly, as she helped Sally unload sheets and covers from an old-fashioned blanket box that doubled as a window seat in the little bedroom. In spite of its size, it was gay with cheerful wallpaper and sparkling white paint and there were pretty turquoise curtains at the window.

'Here's Jason with your stuff,' said Sally, tucking in a corner of the bedspread. 'Give him a hand while I empty a couple of drawers for you.'

Catriona went back reluctantly into the living room in time to see Jason depositing her guitar case on the floor beside the table. Her rucksack was there already, and so were a pile of silver dress boxes marked with the name of the store they had visited the day before.

'I think there's some mistake,' Catriona said quickly.

'What have I forgotten?' He straightened, eyeing her.

Catriona pointed at the boxes. 'They don't belong to me.'

'Don't be a fool,' he said curtly. 'Of course they're yours. What earthly use could they be to me? And don't say I could give them to one of "my women" or I swear I'll turn you across my knee and give you the hiding you've been asking for since I met you.'

'I wasn't going to say that,' she said quietly. 'But I can't accept these clothes. You must see that. I—I can't afford to pay for them just now either, as you know. I only took them to begin with because I thought that . . .' her voice trailed away miserably.

'You thought Jeremy would pay for them as your husband,' he finished for her. 'But as I told you, it's in the family. Of course——' his voice took on that drawling note she had come to dread—'if you insist on repaying me in some other way, I'm sure we can come to some arrangement.'

'Please don't,' she said with difficulty. 'I want to thank you for everything, and you don't make it easy.'

'I don't make it easy for myself either,' he answered abruptly. He came over and stood looking down at her. 'Thank me, then,' he said, smiling faintly.

She lowered her eyes hurriedly to the faded pattern on the carpet. 'I'm much obliged to you,' she said eventually.

Jason gave a swift, impatient sigh. 'Don't be,' he said brusquely. 'I'm sure Cinderella would never have said that to Bluebeard. Goodbye, Catriona. Keep in touch.' And he was gone.

'Now you see him, now you don't,' said Sally cheerfully from the doorway. 'Old Moira will certainly have to go some, if she intends pinning him down for life.'

'Moira?'

'Of course you don't know. Stupid of me,' Sally sat down on a battered-looking armchair and sighed. 'Moira Dane, I mean. She's playing the lead in the TV play I'm in, and at the moment she's hell-bent on letting us all know it. And now she's got her beady eye on Jason. She's been sticking to him like glue ever since casting.'

'Does he produce plays as well as his other work?' Catriona asked.

'No-o.' Sally looked at her oddly. 'Didn't he explain? Well, perhaps not. Anyway, he's in and out of our rehearsals quite a bit for one reason and another, and I'm afraid one of the reasons could be Moira.'

'I suppose she's very attractive,' Catriona said.

'Absolutely gorgeous. She's a redhead like me, but that's about all we have in common. We're supposed to be sisters in the play, so our colouring had to be similar, I suppose,' Sally said. 'It's a marvellous chance for me as long as I don't let Moira goad me into walking out or anything daft.'

'Is she that bad?' Catriona was sympathetic.

'She gets us all down at times—except Jason. He doesn't let anyone, especially a woman, get to him to that extent,' Sally said. 'But she can be really nasty. I suppose she's the sort who would stand on your foot if she thought you had a corn.' She got up briskly. 'Now, I have a rehearsal in about an hour. I'd better show you our splendid kitchen.' She whisked back a gingham curtain in one corner to reveal a miniature sink and cooker crammed into an alcove. 'Food in left-hand cupboard, under fridge. Soap, cleaning stuff and everything else in the other one. Any questions?'

'Is there any room for them?' Catriona laughed.

'Not really,' Sally twinkled back at her. 'I am glad you're here. Are you going to have a few days' sightseeing and general enjoyment before you look for a job? I should.'

Catriona looked at her doubtfully. 'If that's all right.'

'Of course it is. I'll try and get you a pass to see round the TV centre too. Perhaps you could watch the dress rehearsal for the play. I'm sure Hugo wouldn't mind—he's the producer. I'll mention it to him.'

45

'I don't want to be any trouble——' Catriona began diffidently, and Sally grinned at her.

'That's not what Jason said about you on the phone this morning. He said you were a permanent thorn in his flesh—a little Scottish thistle.'

'And he,' said Catriona clearly, 'is quite the most arrogant, detestable—creature I've ever met.'

'That's because you haven't met Moira,' said Sally.

CHAPTER THREE

THE rest of the week passed in a buzz of sightseeing for Catriona. To Sally's amusement she bought a guide book and settled down to visit all the places that had hitherto been only names to her.

'The Tower?' Sally gasped. 'I've never been there, and I've lived within twenty miles of London all my life.'

'Then you should be ashamed,' Catriona told her with mock severity. 'It's a fascinating place—all those stones steeped in history. Just think of all the suffering that's gone on there down the centuries, the tears and blood that have been spilled there.'

'There's enough blood and tears at the TV centre to last me for a while,' said Sally with a groan. 'Keep up the good work, darling, and I'll try and make it to the Zoo with you at least. I can't resist the bears.'

Under Sally's guidance, Catriona had made one or two modest additions to her wardrobe and a dark green trouser suit with a sleeveless tunic top had proved a favourite buy. Sally had shown her too how to blow-dry her hair into the style she had worn at the party and encouraged her to experiment with cosmetics in the day-time as well.

She had put the boxes with the evening gown and other

articles on top of the wardrobe, and to her relief Sally had never questioned her about them.

Nor did she hear from Jason Lord, although he had told her, 'Keep in touch.' It was one of those meaningless phrases, like his perpetual 'darling', she told herself. For the first few days, she had tensed each time the phone rang, but it had always been for Sally, and Catriona found herself in the odd position of not knowing whether she felt glad or sorry. She could tell herself vehemently that if she never saw Jason Lord again, it would be too soon, and yet at the same time it was not pleasant, she found, to be completely ignored.

She was homesick too in many ways. The air of London felt thick after the sparkling clarity of Torvaig with its sea and heather-laden breezes. The anonymity of the place distressed her too, coming from a closely knit community where a kindly interest was expressed in one's most mundane doings. Catriona soon gave up searching the faces of the people she passed in the street for some trace of friendly recognition.

Above all, she missed the sunsets and the blazing jewel colours that used to herald twilight over the western sea. Aunt Jessie had told her when she was a child that it was possible to pick up amethysts and sapphires in the hill burns, and Catriona had been convinced for a long time that these jewels were really pieces that had broken off the sunsets and been washed ashore by the whispering tide.

Jeremy and she had spent one rainy day wading in one of the burns looking for precious stones, she recalled with a pang. But they had found nothing, which made the little ring he had bought her in Fort William doubly precious. She still wore it on the chain round her neck because she could not think what else to do with it. To wear it openly was out of the question, but she could not bear to throw it away either.

Sometimes at night, when the noise of the traffic came

47

between her and sleep, a sudden wave of misery would sweep over her, and she would cry into her pillow, fearful of waking Sally. In a way she welcomed the tears. She felt this continual longing for Jeremy proved that Jason Lord was wrong with his cynical remarks about the transitory nature of first love, although why she felt it necessary to justify her emotions in this way was something she did not probe too deeply.

Sometimes, as she wandered alone among crowded art galleries and museums, she let herself daydream that Jeremy was with her. Once in fact she had stepped through a doorway in the National Gallery and seen him standing there, his back to her, studying a catalogue. It was only when she ran to him and touched his arm and a stranger's face turned and stared down at her that she realised her mistake and stepped back blushing hotly.

She still could not believe he was entirely lost to her. Money had never seemed all important to him during their time together in Scotland. And if that was all that was binding him to Helen, he could still be brought to see that he was making a tragic mistake.

Jason had been right about one thing at least, she recalled, wincing. If she had not seen Jeremy and Helen together at the party, she would never have believed it.

Sometimes she wondered guiltily what Aunt Jessie would have said if she had known her niece was hankering after a man who was openly pledged to another girl. Aunt Jessie had always regarded an engagement as being as binding as the marriage itself, and had clicked her tongue disapprovingly over the feckless modern habit of breaking engagements without a backward glance.

Catriona supposed this was why she still thought of Jeremy as belonging to herself rather than to Helen. The little ring that still lay between her breasts had been a symbol of something she thought would last for ever.

She told herself things would improve when she got a job

and had more to occupy her mind. And she was soon to start work. Sally had taken her along to the agency she used herself between acting jobs, and Catriona blessed the long evenings when Aunt Jessie had shown her typing and the intricacies of book-keeping while she was still a schoolgirl. She had been given a typing test at the agency and had impressed Miss Shaw, the supervisor, with her speed and accuracy.

Miss Shaw looked Catriona over and nodded as if she was satisfied about something.

'What sort of a job are you looking for, Miss Muir?' she inquired. 'A temporary post to start with—or would you prefer something with a degree of permanence about it?' She began to go through a card index file. 'There is something here, as a matter of fact, that I feel might suit you. The Henderson Trust is looking for a general office assistant.'

'Is it a big organisation?' Catriona asked a little apprehensively.

Miss Shaw's eyes twinkled. 'On the contrary, my dear. The Henderson Trust was set up only a few years ago to provide a hostel for homeless people of all kinds. If you took the post, you would be working at the hostel itself for the director, Mr Milner.'

'He may want someone with qualifications,' Catriona said dubiously.

'I don't think you'll find him too exacting,' Miss Shaw promised her. 'Most girls seem to want glamour jobs these days—air-conditioning and luncheon vouchers—and I'm afraid the Trust doesn't fall into that category at all. The money isn't quite as much as a City office would pay either, but I have a feeling that you might find it congenial, and it will help you find your feet a little if nothing else.'

She gave Catriona a green card to present at the Trust at nine o'clock the following Monday morning and wished her luck.

Catriona thought Sally had forgotten her offer to show her round the TV centre, but she was mistaken. Sally raised the subject while they were washing up one evening.

'We're having a complete run-through tomorrow with full sets and costumes prior to recording,' she said. 'I spoke to Hugo and he said you could come as long as you were quiet as a mouse.'

'What did you say?' Catriona smiled, secretly thrilled at the idea of visiting the studios.

'Oh, I said you were the image of a "wee, sleekit, cow'rin', timorous beastie",' Sally responded, grinning. 'Rehearsal starts at one-thirty, so we can have a good look round beforehand. And we're having lunch there,' she added. 'By special invitation.'

'Oh. From whom?' Catriona asked, intrigued.

'Can't you guess?' Sally looked surprised. 'Oh, come off it, love. It's Jason, of course. Who else could it be?'

Catriona felt stricken. She was aware that her face had flushed, and that Sally was looking at her in amazement.

'Do we—have to?' she asked in a low voice.

'Well, yes—no. I mean, I don't see how we can get out of it.' Sally was obviously perplexed. 'I'm sorry, love, I thought you'd enjoy it. I thought you were friends.'

'That's not the word I'd have used,' Catriona said drily.

'Oh dear.' Sally looked downcast. 'I've never probed, but he did bring you here, so I assumed . . .'

'I can guess,' Catriona said a trifle shakily. 'But it was never anything like that, Sally. I—I swear it wasn't.'

'Well, I'll believe you,' Sally said cheerfully. 'But I honestly don't see how we can dodge round this lunch. I'm a struggling actress, after all, and it is his . . .' She stopped, red-faced, and went on hurriedly, 'He is an important producer.'

Catriona wondered what Sally had intended to say, but decided with a mental shrug not to pursue the point. Instead she sighed and said, 'Don't worry, Sally. I can stand one lunch, I suppose. Just as long as I don't have to be alone with him.'

Sally gaped at her. 'Well, you must be alone in feeling that,' she said at last. 'I can't think of any other girl I know who wouldn't give anything to be alone with Jason Lord.'

Catriona smiled wryly. 'Perhaps that's why,' she said, more lightly than she felt.

She was still on edge the next day as she and Sally walked the short distance from the underground station to the massive glass and concrete complex that was Home Counties Television.

At the same time, she was conscious she was looking her best in a scarlet two-piece with a pleated skirt and short-sleeved jacket worn over a white silk shirt. Jason Lord would find her very different from the shabby waif who had arrived so unexpectedly on his doorstep, or who had masqueraded in borrowed plumage at his behest, she thought, her firm little chin jutting defiantly.

She felt less confident when the time came to pass the two security men on the door, but they waved the two girls through with only a cursory glance at their passes.

'We'll go up to Drama first so that I can drop these things off,' Sally remarked as they waited for the lift, indicating the small cream-coloured vanity case she was carrying.

Catriona felt an immediate stir of interest. The plays she had watched over the past week or so were some of the things she had enjoyed most on television, and she was keenly looking forward to seeing Sally in her new role. She had read the script and cued Sally with some of her lines, so she was quite familiar with the story.

'It's about the strain on a family when the elder of the two daughters suddenly returns home for her younger sister's wedding to an old flame of hers,' Sally had explained. 'It's a powerful piece of writing, but it has quite a strong vein of humour in it too.'

51

'Who wrote it?' Catriona asked, idly glancing at the title page.

'Oh, it's a complete unknown, writing his first play,' Sally said, a little hesitantly. 'They call him Jon Lisle.'

'What's wrong?' Catriona glanced at her, puzzled. 'It's not some deadly secret, is it?'

'Of course not.' Sally gave her arm a reassuring squeeze. 'It's just that he doesn't seem to want any personal publicity, that's all.'

Now, as they went up in the lift, Catriona said musingly, 'I wonder if he'll be there.'

'Who?' said Sally.

'Your shy Mr Lisle. I'd love to meet him, Sally, just to tell him how good I think his play is. Surely he wouldn't mind that.'

'We-ell,' Sally frowned a little. 'If I see him, I'll introduce you, I promise. How about that?'

'That'll be great,' Catriona agreed, her eyes shining.

She was keenly interested in everything she saw when they emerged from the lift. As well as a large studio, where the sets for Sally's play were waiting, there were make-up rooms and a bustling wardrobe department.

'Generally we're allowed to wear clothes of our own choosing,' Sally told her. 'The main thing the wardrobe is supplying for me this time is my wedding dress.'

Catriona was introduced to a tall balding man in a baggy navy sweater with large holes in the elbows who turned out to be rather surprisingly the director, Hugo Desmond. If he was not entirely as Catriona had imagined a dynamic television executive to be, she had to admit he had a most charming smile and a wonderful deep voice.

'Don't be deceived. Hugo appears to be very gentle, but he can bellow like an ox when he's angry,' Sally said wryly.

The next hour or so was taken up with looking over the rest of the centre. Catriona was introduced to so many people that she promptly lost track of most of their names and faces as soon as they moved on. She regretted in many ways that she could not share some of her excitement with her friends in Torvaig, but they saw so little television—there was a set at the manse which worked irregularly—that her experiences would mean little to them.

One disappointment was a good-looking young newscaster she had made a point of watching each evening.

'He's much smaller than I imagined—and different,' she said rather sadly to Sally, who smiled understandingly.

'It's an unreal world, I'm afraid,' she said, with a slight wave at their surroundings. 'We're just creators of illusion half the time.' She glanced past Catriona and her pretty face hardened. 'And talking of creations, here comes Moira.'

Catriona longed to turn and stare, but she kept herself strictly under control. She was glad she had, when a husky and very feminine voice said from beside her, 'I thought Hugo had placed an embargo on sightseers, Miss Fenton.'

Moira Dane was tall, with a figure just bordering on voluptuousness, becomingly encased in a black velvet trouser suit. Her violet eyes examined Catriona minutely, then dismissed her as an obvious nonentity.

'I don't think he intended a complete ban, Miss Dane,' Sally replied smoothly. 'He just got a little annoyed with visitors at every rehearsal.'

A faint colour rose in Moira's cheeks.

'Well, I'm glad he's being a little more reasonable,' she said with a shrug. 'As it happens I'm meeting a cousin of mine for lunch, and I'm sure she'd like to watch the run-through as well as your little friend.'

Her last inflection had an unmistakably questioning note, and Sally hastened to repair the omission by performing formal introductions.

'Catriona Muir?' Moira repeated. 'Now I do believe I've heard that name somewhere before. I wonder where it could have been.'

'You must be thinking of someone else, Miss Dane,'

53

Catriona said steadily. 'I only arrived in London last week.'

'Nevertheless——' Moira shrugged again. 'It will come back to me eventually. Things always do.'

'No doubt,' Sally said shortly. 'Well, you must excuse us now. We're lunching too.' And she swept Catriona away.

'Does Hugo really dislike visitors?' Catriona asked anxiously once they were out of earshot. Sally grinned a little.

'He doesn't care for Moira's visitors very much,' she retorted. 'They won't keep quiet during scenes, and they do incredible things like asking Jan the production assistant to bring them coffee. Hugo got good and mad and said he wasn't providing free entertainment for gaping onlookers any more, but he was very sweet when I asked if you could come along.'

Catriona felt relieved, but at the same time she knew the concession had not pleased Moira, and she hoped their paths would not cross again during the afternoon's important rehearsal.

The studio canteen facilities were housed on the top floor of the building. There was a cafeteria section at one end, partitioned off from the restaurant which had waitress service.

Both sections were already quite crowded when they arrived, but Sally led the way unhesitatingly across the thick carpet with its brilliant geometrical pattern in red, gold and black.

'Mr Lord's table, Molly,' she told the waitress who came to meet them, and they were shown at once to a reserved place by the window. There was a breathtaking view over the city and Catriona was soon trying to spot landmarks and find the blue ribbon of the Thames winding its way in the distance.

'Oh, Sally, I've never enjoyed myself so much in my life,' she said impulsively, turning to look at her friend, who was giving the menu the same kind of rapt attention she had been paying the landscape. 'The only blot on it is having to be nice to that Lord man.'

'Well, don't let that spoil your day,' a voice she knew only too well chipped in curtly, and Jason Lord swung himself into the third chair at the table. 'You've never allowed good manners to stand in the way before, Miss Muir—why bother now?'

Catriona was blushing to the roots of her hair. She had been guilty of a piece of schoolgirlish rudeness, and had been well repaid for it.

'I didn't know you were there,' she managed at last.

'I'm sure you didn't.' He handed her a menu. 'What's your pleasure, Miss Muir—or do you prefer another bite at the hand that intends to feed you?'

'Stop teasing her, Jason,' Sally said chidingly. 'You know what they say about eavesdroppers, anyway.'

'Oh, I'm used to hearing no good of myself, aren't I, Cinderella?' He smiled at Catriona, who glared back at him, hating the memories the nickname invoked.

Sally laid down her menu. 'You choose for us, Jason. And just remember that wedding dress is a tight fit even when I've had no lunch!'

'Okay. How does prawn cocktail, followed by a steak and green salad, sound?'

'Fine,' said Sally immediately. Catriona wanted to reject the suggested meal out of hand, but she was hungry and anxious not to upset Sally, so she murmured something acquiescent and stared at the pattern in the damask cloth until the first course arrived.

Jason appeared to ignore her silence, turning instead to Sally with talk on topics to do with their work in television. In spite of herself Catriona began to watch him covertly as they ate. He was wearing a blue denim shirt with the sleeves rolled casually back to reveal tanned forearms. A broad leather belt fastened his matching hipster pants. He was far more casually dressed than any other man in the room, and, she was forced to admit to herself, by far the most attractive too.

Just then Sally bent to get a handkerchief from her bag, and Jason, lounging in his chair, turned to Catriona. Their eyes met for one challenging instant, and she felt that odd shiver of awareness curl down her backbone. Although she had been forced into a situation of unexpected intimacy with him, he was still very much an unknown quantity, she realised. She could not believe that firm, rather thin-lipped mouth had touched hers, even in pretence. There was something completely inimical between them, she thought. They had disliked each other on sight, although she had been forced to be grateful to him in a number of ways since. But that did not mean she had to like him any the better, she told herself.

'And what have you been doing with yourself?' he asked casually, and she flushed, unwilling to tell him about her sightseeing expeditions.

Sally supplied the answer. 'Oh, Catriona's the complete tourist. I don't know how many pairs of shoes she's worn out tramping from Nelson's Column down to Buckingham Palace and back. But she starts work on Monday, so it'll be weekends only from now on, I'm afraid.'

'Gather ye rosebuds while ye may,' he quoted mockingly. 'Lucky girl, Miss Muir, to be visiting London for the first time. We tend to forget how exciting it can be. Are you fond of excitement?' The grey eyes held hers with a kind of veiled insolence.

'If it's the right sort of excitement—yes,' Catriona answered quietly.

'Ah.' He pushed his empty plate away and studied her face. 'But what is the right sort? Mightn't you have to sample the wrong sort as well before you can find out?'

His eyes travelled over her again, and she experienced once more that curious urge to shield herself with her hands.

Sally broke in impatiently, 'Well, I hope you both know

what you're talking about, because I'm blowed if I do. Ask the waitress to bring the trolley, Jason. I'm going to have a meringue, and to hell with the wedding dress.'

Catriona was thankful to be spared Jason's undivided attention, and she made a mental resolution to keep out of his way from now on. She found him far too disturbing in a way she could not comprehend.

She was just finishing her slice of raspberry tart with whipped cream when Moira Dane's voice exclaimed, 'Darling! So this is where you got to.'

She bent to kiss Jason's lean cheek.

'You're absolutely wicked,' she went on. 'I left all sorts of urgent messages at Reception about lunch today.'

'A prior engagement.' Jason took her hand and laid its palm to his mouth. 'Anyway, I thought my attraction for you only began after the hours of darkness.'

'Honestly!' Moira gave a little giggle like oozing honey. 'You'll shock poor Helen.'

Up to then, Catriona had paid little heed to Moira's companion. She had been too involved trying to sort out her own unexpectedly mixed feelings at the interruption and Jason's attitude to the woman who bent so intimately over him. It was not difficult to guess their relationship, she thought. What had he said? That he didn't take sweets from babies. Well, Moira Dane was certainly a very grown-up lady, and if Jason was availing himself of any sweets that were going, it was certainly nothing to do with her.

But now, with a start, she recognised the fair-haired girl being introduced to Sally. It was Jeremy's fiancée whom she had glimpsed so briefly but so drastically at the party. For a moment panic welled up inside her, then she felt Jason's eyes on her, bleak with warning.

'And this is Miss Catriona Muir,' Moira turned to her. 'A great friend of your future in-laws—or some of them, at least.'

Catriona put down her coffee cup with a sick feeling. She

realised fatalistically that Helen must be the cousin that Moira had spoken of earlier, and by the malicious look the two of them had just exchanged it seemed as if Jeremy had been more than frank with his fiancée about his relationships before his engagement.

'It's a small world,' Jason drawled into the awkward silence. He rose and shook hands with Helen, who was peeping rather coyly at him through heavily mascaraed lashes. 'I'm sorry we didn't meet the other evening, Helen, but there were such crowds around you, I thought I'd save that pleasure for a rather more private occasion.'

His slightly raised brows and the smile he gave her implied that he did not consider the present occasion private enough either, and Helen gave him a conscious smile.

'Jeremy did tell me about his wicked uncle. I see what he meant,' she said archly, and Jason laughed.

Catriona suddenly felt an overwhelming urge to escape. 'I think we'd better be going——' she began, reaching for her bag. As she did so her sleeve caught her half-filled cup and knocked it over, spilling the contents on to the white cloth.

'Oh dear! What a mess,' Moira said lightly, as Catriona, hot with embarrassment, pushed her chair back and stood up.

'Oh, love, it hasn't spoiled your clothes?' Sally said sympathetically, and Catriona shook her head, trying to regain her composure.

'What a fuss about a little accident,' Jason commented sardonically. 'Run away if you wish, Miss Muir, but they don't hang people for spilling coffee, you know.'

He seemed to take a positive delight in making her feel gauche, she thought furiously, and turned on him with her green eyes flashing, but before she could speak, he laughed easily and took her arm.

'Come on, darling. I'll show you the office where I get all my inspiration. Sally has to go to Make-up now and you'll only be in the way. Isn't that right, Sal? Goodbye, Helen. I look forward to having you as a niece. See you later, Moira.'

And he walked away casually, his fingers tight as bands round Catriona's wrist.

'Don't make a scene here,' he murmured. 'My room's soundproof, and you can let off steam in there.' He paused to sign the bill the waitress brought him, then continued a leisurely progress to the door, answering greetings from other diners as he went.

As they waited for the lift outside the restaurant, he produced a pack of American cigarettes from the pocket of his shirt and lit one. Catriona stood massaging her wrist where the marks of his fingers clearly showed and maintained a hostile silence.

'Remind me to type out a quote for you before you leave,' he remarked as the lift began to descend. 'It's the one about tangled webs and deception.'

'You need not bother yourself. I know it already,' Catriona said stormily.

'Then you'll agree it's apt.' He allowed her to precede him out of the lift. 'My office is down here on the left.'

'And it can stay there!' Catriona retorted, knowing that she was being childish but too angry to care much. 'I'm going to find Sally.'

'Not now,' he said decisively, and took her hand again. 'She has to get ready and Hugo's tolerance of spectators is limited. I'll take you up to the studio before the rehearsal gets under way. In you go.'

He pushed open a door and Catriona glared helplessly at him for a moment before entering the room.

It was not a large room and the main item was a desk, seething in papers. There was a portable typewriter, pushed to one side, jostling with several telephones and an intercom system. A shelf overflowed with books, mostly of a reference nature, she noticed, and two filing cabinets stood in gleaming splendour against one wall. An expensive leather coat was flung over the only spare chair—a low black leather and chrome affair. Jason picked up the coat and slung it casually in the general direction of an empty coat-stand in the corner.

'Take a seat,' he invited, and flicked a switch on the intercom. 'Two coffees, Diane.'

'Not for me,' Catriona protested immediately.

'Oh, stop arguing. You spilled most of yours and you could do with some kind of stimulant. You look like a ghost,' he observed a little cruelly. 'It seems to be my fate to be around you at moments of crisis. I'd hoped to meet you in a relaxed mood today.'

'You hoped to meet me?' She stared at him in frank disbelief.

'Why not?' He glanced at her, his brows raised, then came to sit on the edge of the desk. 'You're very attractive, Miss Muir, as I'm sure you know. I'm also sure you have hidden charms as well—if ever you allow anyone close enough to discover them.'

'I consider you've been quite close enough,' she said, her voice shaking a little.

'Oh?' He stubbed out his cigarette in a huge onyx ash tray. 'Because I once kissed you and removed your dress— not simultaneously?'

Catriona stared at him, her face crimson. 'I wonder you're not ashamed to remember that.'

'Shame has never featured very high among my emotions,' he told her drily, as the door opened and a tall dark girl wearing huge tinted glasses came in carrying a tray of coffee. There was silence as Catriona helped herself to sugar, and refused the biscuits that were provided with a shake of her head. Then Diane left the room after a quiet word of thanks from Jason.

It was Jason who spoke first once they were alone again. 'I like your outfit.'

It was on the tip of her tongue to tell him she'd had no

60

thought of him when she put it on, but then she remembered what she had been thinking when she arrived that morning and bit back the retort with a slightly raised colour.

'You blush delightfully too,' he went on smoothly. 'I confess I'd forgotten girls still could at your age. How old did you say you were?'

'I didn't say,' she said curtly. 'But I'm twenty.'

'You look younger,' he said briefly, swallowing some coffee. 'Especially when you sulk.'

'I am not sulking——' Catriona began indignantly, then stopped, realising how ridiculous such an argument could only become.

'All right,' he held up a mocking hand. 'We'll call a truce. I don't want to figure as the villain of the piece on your day out. Are you enjoying it, and have you seen everything that you wanted?'

'I'm looking forward to seeing the play later on,' she admitted. 'It's a good story, and I think Sally is going to be tremendous.'

'I think so too. I've a lot of time for young Sal,' he said. 'You two get on all right?'

'Isn't it obvious?'

'Obvious conclusions aren't always the correct ones,' he returned.

'Yes, I like her very much.'

'I'm pleased,' Jason said coolly. 'After all, you have a lot in common, or haven't you confided in each other to that extent yet?' Catriona stared at him wide-eyed and he nodded. 'That's right, darling—Jeremy, of course. Although Sal managed to get out heart-whole,' he added.

'I had no idea,' Catriona said numbly.

'Does it make any difference?' he asked. 'It certainly hasn't to Sally. She's fairly shrewd and she soon saw through Jeremy. I thought perhaps if you discussed things with her, you might end up feeling a little less sorry for yourself.'

'I haven't discussed it with anyone. It's not something

61

I'm particularly anxious to have known,' Catriona said quietly.

He shrugged. 'As you wish. But this isn't really what I brought you here to talk about.' He paused. 'Do you remember saying you intended to repay me for the dress and other stuff?'

'Yes.' Catriona looked at him a little apprehensively. 'But I don't start work until Monday and . . .'

He raised his hand again, silencing her. 'I don't mean money,' he told her, his smile widening as he took in her instant look of alarm and the instinctive stiffening of her slender body. 'And I don't mean what you seem to think, either. Making love can be a gift—but never the repayment of a debt. I'm afraid what I have in mind is far more prosaic. How are you at housework?'

Catriona was too taken aback to answer for a minute. Jason paused, obviously expecting some response, then gave a little impatient sigh.

'I ask, because you could help me out of a real jam, if you wanted,' he said. 'Mrs Birch, poor soul, has slipped and fallen at home and sprained her wrist. She'll be out of action for some time and the flat is chaos without her.' He paused again and eyed Catriona. 'I can't do without a woman around, I suppose—even if not for the purpose you seem to suspect.'

'Can I get this straight?' she demanded, her voice quivering a little. 'You want me to come and clean your flat for you every day?'

'Oh, not as often as that,' he said hastily. 'But if you could pop round and straighten up for me until I can make alternative arrangements, I'd be grateful. But if you think the suggestion is an insult . . .'

'Oh, no,' Catriona said quickly. 'I'd be glad to do it. I'm quite used to housework. It would be no bother at all.'

'Then it's a bargain. Consider all debts paid in full.' He

slid off the desk and held out his hand, his eyes compelling her to return the gesture. She rose in turn and touched his fingers awkwardly, wishing that she did not find the slightest physical contact with him such a disturbing experience.

'It doesn't seem right, though,' she said, her forehead puckered slightly. 'The dress cost such a lot and this is so little to do in return.'

'So little?' he echoed mockingly. 'I can't think of one other girl I know that I'd care to ask—or trust to do it. And you don't have to worry about having to endure my company for two days running,' he added abruptly. 'I shall be here at the studio all day. You can get on in your own way and eat when you feel like it. There's masses of food in the fridge. Mrs Birch stocked up just before her accident.'

'Thank you,' Catriona said, feeling foolish. For a moment her imagination had created a scene she did not care to contemplate of Jason working in his study, while she cleaned and prepared meals and made coffee. It was somehow a more intimate picture than the night she had spent in the flat.

'I shall be gone by half past eight. Can you manage that, or shall I leave the key with the other tenants?' he asked.

'I'll be there before you leave,' she assured him. 'Will I find everything in the kitchen?'

'Yes, I'll show you round before I leave. I know where everything is even if I'm not much good at using it,' he said, grinning. 'There are some rubber gloves as well, I think.'

'Oh, I never use the silly things,' she said, speaking more lightly than she had felt inclined to do in his presence previously.

'No.' He reached out deliberately and took her hand again, studying the small rounded palm and slim fingers. 'This is a working hand all right.' He traced one of its lines with his fingertip. 'This is your heart line, Catriona. It looks remarkably steady. I don't see Jeremy on it, do you?'

Catriona wanted to pull away, but instead she stood gazing down at the floor while the silence between them became almost tangible.

'Catriona.' His voice was low, and the teasing note was still there but subtly altered in some strange way. 'Shall I tell the studio to go to hell and stay at home tomorrow?'

'Aren't you forgetting? Lovemaking is no way to pay a debt,' she flung at him almost wildly, shocked at her own reactions. Had she forgotten who he was and his utter ruthlessness in getting what he wanted? Besides, she still loved Jeremy, she told herself desperately, so why this sudden traitorous longing to feel Jason's body hard with desire against hers, his mouth irrevocably dissolving her shyness away?

He released her hand abruptly, and she flinched from the anger in his eyes.

'I thought we'd agreed the debt was paid,' he said. 'Don't worry, Catriona. I won't ask you to pay again.'

The intercom sounded and Diane's voice said, 'The studio have rung down, Mr Lord.'

'Fine.' He switched the machine off, and turned to Catriona. 'That was Hugo's all-clear. We can go up now.'

'Are you going to watch the run-through too?'

'Why, yes,' he said coolly. 'I too have an interest in this play, you know.'

Catriona supposed he meant Moira Dane. The actress had made it clear in the restaurant that there had been more than mere friendship between them. Well, Catriona thought bitterly, she would not add to the lists of his conquests, no matter what tricks his experience with other women had taught him.

'Well, come on,' Jason said impatiently, his hand on the doorhandle. 'This is what you came here for after all, isn't it?'

But as she followed him to the lift, Catriona found herself wondering if that was now altogether true.

Somewhat to her surprise, she thoroughly enjoyed the rehearsal that followed. She sat with Jason but not near him in the producer's box. Hugo and his assistants sat at a control panel in front of a bank of television screens, communicating with the cast and floor manager through microphones.

In spite of her instinctive dislike of Moira, Catriona had to admit she was a fine actress. She was playing a basically unsympathetic character, but she managed to invest it with a kind of pathetic dignity at the end. Sally's role as the younger girl could have been insipid by contrast, but was saved by the excellence of the writing, Catriona realised, as well as Sally's very good performance. She was sorry when the play reached its ironic climax and Hugo called for a break.

He came over to her and smiled kindly. 'Enjoy it?' he asked, and she nodded mutely.

'If you want to pop up to the canteen for a coffee, now's your chance. Sally has to go along to Wardrobe to get something done about that damn silly train they've given her and I want to run through a few things again. Can you manage to find your way up there on your own?'

Catriona assured him that she could. For one heart-stopping moment, she was afraid that Jason would accompany her. He held the studio door open for her as she left, but to her relief went off in the opposite direction without a word.

Catriona decided to use the cafeteria this time. She collected a coffee and a portion of gateau and carried them to an empty table. Unlike the restaurant, this part of the room was furnished with tables covered in a teak laminate with comfortable bench seats on each side.

The cafeteria was barely half full, and Catriona amused herself by seeing how many people she could recognise from her brief acquaintance with television. She was trying to place one short fair man whom she associated with a panel game of some kind when Moira's voice said, 'May we join you?'

Catriona looked up, startled. Moira had a young man with her this time. His light brown hair was even longer than Jason's and he wore a rather Victorian-looking moustache. His suit was a pale coffee colour, and his shirt was brown and gold with a matching tie.

'This is Roger Hunt,' Moira said carelessly as they sat down. 'He's a columnist with the *Evening Globe*.'

This meant little to Catriona, but she smiled politely and shook hands with him, a little confused by the openly admiring look he gave her. But his manner was pleasant and after a few moments in his company she began to feel quite relaxed.

'You haven't much of an accent for a Scots lass,' he commented.

'Well, my mother was English and my father spent most of his time south of the Border,' Catriona answered. 'Besides, we don't spend all our time saying "Och" and "havers", you know.'

'Oh, I'm not criticising. Your voice is delightful with that faint underlying lilt,' he said.

Catriona was not used to quite so personal remarks from a stranger and she drank some coffee to mask her growing embarrassment.

'How long have you been in London, Catriona? I may call you that?'

'I suppose so,' she said, wondering why he should want to. After all, they were never likely to meet again. 'And I've only been in London a short while,' she added, faltering a little as she met Moira's speculative gaze. That was the trouble with telling lies, she reflected miserably. You had to remember exactly what you'd said, long after it had ceased to matter. What had she told Jeremy? She knew she had given him the impression that she and Jason were well acquainted. And what had he told Helen, for her in turn to pass on to Moira? The whole thing was turning into a crazy spiral to disaster, she thought dazedly.

'Well, you've been a busy girl for a comparative new-comer,' Roger Hunt said, tracing the design on his saucer with an idle finger. 'Jason Lord's scalp isn't bad going for a country mouse.'

'Scalp?' Catriona stared at him indignantly. 'I don't know what you mean.'

'Oh, come off it, love. You're not going to give me that "just good friends" routine, are you?'

Catriona felt increasingly bewildered. 'Good friends' was hardly how she would have described any part of her relationship with Jason, she thought.

'I don't know what you've heard,' she began. 'But I can assure you . . .'

'Oh, we've heard enough,' he said lightly. 'Don't look so overcome, sweetie. After all, this is swinging London and not Ben Cockaleekie, or wherever you come from. So you're shacked up with Jason Lord for a while. It happens.

'Besides,' he went on, during the small shocked pause while Catriona tried to collect her whirling thoughts, 'No one blames you. I wish I had whatever it is Jason's got. I've never been the irresistible type.'

'But it wasn't like that,' Catriona broke in urgently. 'It was only one night, and that was all a mistake . . .'

He laughed, and Moira joined in with a forced air, her eyes veiled behind her incredibly long lashes as she watched Catriona floundering.

'Your mistake, petal, certainly not Jason's. How does he do it?' and he whistled appreciatively.

'No!' Catriona felt as if she was in a nightmare. Somehow she had to explain, but without mentioning the part Jeremy had played in all this. Moira and Helen would have no more to gloat over.

67

'You see, I got myself stupidly stranded,' she tried again. 'Jason found out and offered to put me up for the night. It was very kind of him—and that's all there was to it,' she added with a touch of desperation as the pair opposite her continued to smile.

Moira leaned forward. 'Tell me, Miss Muir, was this before or after you appeared at his nephew's engagement party wearing a Corelli model? Who supplied that, I wonder?'

'Well, he did, but I'm paying for it.'

'Well, that's a new twist.' Moira produced a jewelled holder from her bag and began to fit a cigarette into it. 'It doesn't really match with the picture of Jason as a pattern of chivalry offering shelter to homeless damsels either.'

'But he did—and now I'm doing his housework for him while his housekeeper is away ill,' Catriona said all in a rush, and was rewarded with complete silence from her two interrogators.

Roger Hunt's eyes were round with almost comical surprise. 'Incredible,' he commented at last. 'It's so way out, it must be true, and it gets better and better.' He turned to Moira, who sat stony-eyed, puffing rather jerkily at her cigarette. 'I think our nasty suspicions have done this lovely creature an injustice, my darling. We thought she was Jason's latest fancy and she turns out to be the cleaning lady instead. What a disappointment!' He looked at Catriona and smiled. 'When do you put your pinny on, then, love?'

'I start in the morning,' Catriona said wearily. She was at a loss to know how she had ever got involved in all this. All she'd had to do was get up and walk away, she told herself. She hadn't been obliged to answer any of their insulting questions. But at least they knew the truth now, and wouldn't regard her as one of Jason's cast-off mistresses.

'Fine.' Roger drained his cup and glanced at his wristwatch. 'Time I returned you to Hugo, Moira my pet. We'll postpone our little chat to another less fraught occasion. Coming, Catriona?'

'No,' Catriona said steadily. The thought of coming face to face with Jason after what had just happened appalled her. 'I—I think I'll go on home now, if you'd just tell Sally.'

'Of course,' said Moira. She gave Catriona a brittle smile and moved off.

Catriona watched them go. The ugly little encounter had ruined the day for her. And what was Moira's part in all this? Just jealousy—or did she have a particular reason for wanting to know Catriona's exact relationship to Jason?

Riding home on the underground, Catriona had the odd conviction that Moira would have preferred her to admit that she had slept with Jason, and so was firmly in his past and no longer part of the competition.

'As if I ever was,' she thought wryly, and wondered why the reflection was not nearly as comforting as it should have been.

CHAPTER FOUR

CATRIONA didn't have time to feel embarrassed when she arrived at Jason's flat the following morning. She had overslept after a strangely disturbed night and so missed the tube train she had wanted to catch and was forced to wait several minutes for the next.

Jason was waiting in the hall, his leather coat over his shoulders, smoking impatiently.

'So you've come,' he said rather coldly, his eyes going over her, taking in the familiar shabby jeans and the black polo-necked sweater.

'Did you doubt it?' she countered.

'I began to wonder.'

He led the way into the kitchen and gave her a swift briefing on where to find all the things she would be most likely to need.

'Do what you think is necessary,' he told her. 'But don't touch the papers on my desk in the study. I'll sort them myself tonight. And don't take it as a personal affront. Mrs Birch has exactly the same instructions,' he added irritably, as Catriona bit her lip at the harshness in his voice.

'I've written the studio number and my extension on the pad by the phone. Ring if you get into difficulties,' he said, and was gone.

The flat seemed very quiet when she was alone. She wandered around getting acclimatised, and decided to make a start on Jason's bedroom. She found fresh fitted undersheets and pillowcases in the well-stocked linen cupboard and began to strip the big bed. It was a simple task, as the only coverlet was a continental quilt, similar to the one in the other room where she had slept.

Its cover was luxuriously patterned in black and silver and Catriona admired it as she made the bed and patted the quilt into place. She decided she would try her hand at washing the bed linen. Her trips to the launderette with Sally had conquered any misgivings about the automatic washing machine in the kitchen. She collected the bedding, and towels together and looked round for Jason's pyjamas. After she had searched the bathroom for them without success, she realised that he must sleep without them, and the realisation made her feel hot with embarrassment. It was typical of his lack of convention, she thought.

By ten o'clock, the bedrooms and bathroom were sparkling and she was ready to start on the living room. First, she felt she deserved a cup of coffee, but after dubiously eyeing the gleaming electric percolator, she decided to stick to the instant variety that she found in the back of a cupboard. She was just adding milk and sugar to her brew when the door-bell rang. Catriona hesitated. She had not been told how to deal with callers, but on the other hand she was in a way deputising for Mrs Birch, so she marched to the front door and threw it open.

She was amazed to see Roger Hunt and another man standing on the step.

'You!' she commented unwelcomingly.

'Surprise, surprise.' Roger moved forward, his hands tucked into his trouser belt. He gave her a charming grin. 'Are you going to let us in, sweetie?'

'Certainly not.' Catriona made to shut the door, but un-accountably Roger's foot was in the way.

'Oh, come on, love, have a heart,' he said. 'After all, it was you gave me the idea. We're running a feature on pretty girls who earn their livings in—er—unusual ways, and we'd like you to be one of them—if you'll let us use you.'

'Use me?' Catriona stared at him. 'What in the world can you mean?'

'You know.' He sounded impatient. 'A few carefully chosen words—a couple of pictures and a nice little fee for you if we decide to run the piece.'

'Absolutely not!' Catriona was horrified.

'But why? There's no harm,' he urged. 'Just a few minutes of your time, that's all.'

There was a click and Catriona saw that the other man was lowering an efficient-looking camera.

'See—painless,' Roger said airily.

'You had no right to do that!' Catriona flamed.

'Well, you just say the word we want to hear and it will all be above board, won't it,' Roger said calmly. 'Greg and I aren't here to upset you, love. We could help each other. We get a feature, and you get a cheque which probably wouldn't come amiss.'

'But I don't do this for a living,' Catriona protested. 'I start my real job on Monday.'

'You worry too much,' Roger said soothingly. 'There is such a thing as artistic licence, you know. And you're here with your pinny on as promised.'

'If I say yes, will you get it over with and go?' Catriona asked wearily, and he brightened.

'Naturally.' He walked past her into the hall and looked round. 'Nice place, Greg. Lord by nature as well as name, by the look of things.' He turned to Catriona. 'Is that coffee I can smell?'

'I suppose so,' Catriona sighed, pushing her hair back in defeat.

While they were drinking their coffee in the kitchen, she made an excuse and went to Jason's study. It was important to get his agreement to this, she thought as she dialled the number he had left. But when she was put through to his extension, there was a setback in store. Diane answered and told her that Mr Lord was watching the recording of *Under the Skin*, the play Sally was in, and couldn't be disturbed. Catriona put the phone down with another sigh.

Back in the kitchen she submitted to being photographed transferring the washing from the machine to the neighbouring tumble drier, then obediently pretended to vacuum the sitting room carpet. But when Roger decided a bed-making picture was required as well, she rebelled.

'I've already made the beds. It's ridiculous,' she protested.

'Artistic licence, sweetie. I did warn you.' Roger ushered her firmly towards Jason's bedroom where she posed wearily, smoothing the quilt and shaking up the pillows, while she answered questions from Roger on her life in Scotland and her views on London. Then, tilting her chin in a way Mrs McGregor would have recognised, she called a halt.

'I'm supposed to be working, and you've taken up enough of my time,' she said firmly.

Roger lifted a hand. 'And we've a deadline to catch, so

we'll leave you in peace. Thanks for your co-operation, my sweet.' And to Catriona's surprise and annoyance, he kissed her carelessly on the cheek.

'The nerve of him!' she muttered, as she closed the door behind them.

The interruption had held her up for over an hour and a half she realised with annoyance as she set to work again. But by early afternoon, there was only Jason's study left do do, she realised thankfully.

It was an attractive room, carpeted in deep red, the walls lined with shelves of books. The centrepiece was the desk, even more littered with papers than the one at the studio had been, Catriona thought as she vacuumed the floor-length curtains. Though her hands itched to tidy them, she obeyed her instructions implicitly and contented herself with dusting all the other available surfaces instead.

She had just changed the nozzle on the cleaner before starting on the carpet when it happened. As she straightened, the handle of the cleaner caught the corner of the desk and a pile of papers went cascading to the floor.

'Oh no!' Catriona went down on her knees and began to gather them together. As she did so, she noticed at first incuriously and then with growing interest that the sheets she was holding were typed like the pages of dialogue in Sally's script. As she looked more closely, she realised that it was part of a play and she began to read. The scene she had chanced on was a confrontation between a woman and her husband who had just discovered she had been unfaithful to him. The man came across as a boorish individual, and yet as the scene progressed, his grief and hurt came compellingly through. It was powerful stuff, and Catriona was so engrossed she entirely failed to hear the front door opening, and only realised she was no longer alone when the study door swung open and Jason said grimly, 'I thought I asked you not to meddle with anything on that desk.'

Flushing painfully, she scrambled to her feet. 'I didn't

mean to pry,' she said. 'I knocked some of the papers on the floor by accident and started to read as I was picking them up again. I—I couldn't put it down. Please forgive me.'

'There's nothing to forgive,' he said shortly. He held out his hand for the papers and she passed them to him, feeling like a scolded child.

'I didn't know you wrote plays. I thought you only made documentaries and things like that,' she said.

'Nobody knows, except Hugo and the select few.' He saw realisation dawning in her eyes and nodded. 'Yes, you're right. I'm the Jon Lisle whose work you so much admire, according to Sally.' His lips curled a little in a mirthless smile. 'If you'd known it was me, your admiration would have been lessened, no doubt.'

'No, it wouldn't,' she said, facing him. 'I think *Under the Skin* is marvellous and I'm sure everyone else will too. And this one could be even better.'

He came round the desk and took the papers from her. 'Maybe it could at that,' he said, almost absently. He gave her a taut smile. 'The important thing is that no one must know who I am. I want the plays to be judged on their own merits and not for anything I may or may not have done in the past in a totally different field. Can you understand that?'

'Yes, I think so,' Catriona said thoughtfully.

'Then I'm in your hands.' He looked squarely at her. 'What are you going to do?'

'I shan't do anything,' Catriona said, puzzled, then light dawned. 'You mean—you think—that I'll tell everyone!'

'Well, it would be the perfect revenge if you felt you needed one,' he said, lighting a cigarette.

Catriona stared at him helplessly for a moment, then she moved to brush past him and away, tears pricking at her eyelids. He caught her arm in a merciless grip.

'Where do you think you're going?'

She struggled. 'Let me go!'

'Try not to be such a fool,' he said calmly. He pulled her round to face him and studied her. 'What's the matter? Did the suggestion hurt your pride?'

'You had no right to say what you did,' she flared.

'Perhaps not,' Jason agreed. 'I just had to make sure, that was all.'

'Now that you are sure—please may I go?'

'Not yet,' he returned equably. 'Now that my guilty secret is out, and presumably safe with you, you could be a great help to me.' He gestured towards the littered desk. 'It will take me half the night to do this on my own. How about it? Are you a secretary bird as well as a home help?'

Catriona paused for a moment. She could recognise that from Jason Lord this was almost an olive branch and some of her resentment began to fade at the unexpectedness of it.

'I'd like to help,' she agreed quietly.

'Fine.' His voice was equally quiet. 'Shall we get started?'

At first they worked in silence, but gradually Jason began to talk to her about television drama, and the impact he was hoping to make when his play was shown.

'Are you hoping that playwriting will take over from everything else completely one day?' she asked, rather shyly.

He smiled. 'It's too early to say. I'd like some critical reaction to *Under the Skin* before I start looking to the future, though Hugo's seen the first draft of the new play and he seems to like it and want to do it.'

'I don't suppose writing plays makes an awful lot of money either,' Catriona said doubtfully.

His lips quivered slightly. 'Spoken like a canny Scot,' he said. 'But you can forget any romantic visions of me starving in a garret for my art. I have interests in several of my brother's companies, so I do have a source of income apart from my TV work. But at the moment I'm quite heavily committed to my documentary work, so I shan't be coming to any snap decisions.'

'Your brother is much older than you, isn't he?' Catriona ventured.

'Eleven years. I was definitely an afterthought.' He eyed her. 'Planning on becoming an interviewer, Miss Muir? I must find a place for you in my team.'

'Oh no,' she said, blushing fierily and trying to subdue the unwelcome thought that in this softer, almost teasing mood he was devastatingly attractive. She wondered what her re-action would have been if they had simply met as strangers at some social gathering and she had not been forced to regard him as the uncle of the man she loved, then she chided herself for being naïve. If her search for Jeremy had not led her to his flat, their paths would never have crossed. His world was peopled with women like Moira Dane, who knew all the arts of attracting a man's attention.

She watched him covertly as he sorted through a sheaf of papers, frowning a little. He was an entirely different type from Jeremy, she decided, although there was a faint family resemblance. Jeremy's good looks were still boyish in many ways, but Jason Lord looked totally male and totally adult, she thought, studying his firm-lipped, rather sensual mouth, and the uncompromising lines of his cheekbones and jaw. She saw he was glancing at her, his brows raised inquiringly, and hastily dropped her gaze back to the notes in her lap, giving herself a mental kick as she did so.

It was several hours before the desk was finally cleared, and all the papers—typescripts, notes and correspondence, collated and filed in the small cabinet under the window.

Jason straightened with a groan. 'It's time we ate,' he said. His eyes narrowed as he looked at Catriona. 'Did you have any lunch?'

'I forgot,' she admitted, and he sighed in exasperation.

'Right, grab your coat and we'll go out.'

'I can't go out like this,' she protested, indicating her shabby jeans and the high-necked black sweater.

'Why not? They constituted almost your entire wardrobe at one time.'

'I know that,' she said unhappily.

'But it won't do any more, is that it? Oh, country mouse, what have we done to you?' He was silent for a moment. 'Is it really your clothes that are bugging you, or do you not want to repeat the distressing experience of eating in my company?'

She flushed like a peony, remembering the lunch party at the studio. 'It's just my clothes.'

'Then that's easily settled. There's a good Italian place, not far from Sal's. I'll take you there to change first as long as you swear to be quick.'

Swearing it was one thing, performing it quite another, Catriona found as she looked over her small stock of clothes, wondering what to wear. In the end, prompted by Jason's impatient pacings in the living room only a few feet away, she decided on one of her newest purchases, a midi-length skirt in violet wool worn with a white silk blouse with long full sleeves, fastening at the back with a mass of tiny buttons. She thought she had managed to fasten it quite successfully, but when she reached the top she found she had only one buttonhole left for two buttons and had to start again. She had to twist herself to see in the mirror and her arms were beginning to ache as she worked away. She groaned out loud when she realised she had again missed a button almost halfway down.

If only Sally had been there, but she had left a note to say she had gone to the cinema with a friend from drama school days. Catriona began awkwardly to unfasten the blouse again when Jason rapped on the bedroom door.

'What in hell's name are you doing?' he called. 'You've got three minutes to get out here.'

Catriona immediately became all thumbs. 'I'm sorry,' she called back. 'I'm having bother with some buttons and . . .'

Her voice died away in sheer shock as the bedroom door was flung open and Jason stood surveying her.

'My God,' he said disgustedly. 'Is that all?'

He was across the room and fastening them before she could say or do anything to prevent him, and instantly all her old hackles rose. The nerve of him, marching into her room like this without so much as a by your leave! she raged inwardly, standing completely rigid in an attempt to ignore the warmth of his fingers on her bare skin.

'There,' he said as the last button was secured.

'Thank you,' she returned stiffly. 'You're very kind.'

'I'm very hungry,' he said. 'If you'd given me a shout five minutes ago, we could have been eating by now.'

'How foolish of me.' Catriona picked up her bag from the bed and walked to the door. She gave him a cool, sweet smile. 'I'm just not used to having a man to help me dress, I'm afraid.'

'But I thought as I'd once undressed you, you'd make an exception in my case,' he said, and grinned unpleasantly as the colour flared in her cheeks. 'You've a short memory, haven't you, darling? The next time it happens I'll try and make it more memorable for you.'

Mortified tears sparkled on her lashes, as she stared impotently at him. 'I don't know how you can remind me of that awful night,' she said in a low voice. 'I feel nothing but shame when I think of it.'

'Then you're a fool. If anyone should have any regrets, it's myself.'

'What have you to regret?'

'That I let you sleep alone.' His mouth curved sardonically at the sight of her startled face. 'After all, I meant to jolt you out of caring for Jeremy. I might as well have made a good job of it while I was about it.'

'And you really think that one night with you would have —cured me?' If she hadn't been so angry, she could almost have laughed at the insufferable arrogance of this creature,

78

who imagined he was so irresistible to women. 'You flatter yourself, Mr Lord.'

'Do I?' He was beside her and she found herself with her last coherent thought wondering why she had ever thought his eyes wintry when they could glow with such a strange and unfamiliar light . . .

He took her by the hips and pulled her towards him, grinding her body against his own so intimately that she cried out in outrage—a protest instantly stifled as his lips came down on hers.

And what had any kiss she had ever received to do with this achingly sensual exploration of her mouth by his, until tremblingly but inevitably her lips parted to his insistence. For a moment, even then, she tried to rebel as the kiss deepened to a shattering intimacy she had never dreamed of, then blindly, wordlessly, she succumbed, her shaking hands twining themselves in his dark hair.

His hands slid from her hips to her waist, then probed the quivering nerve endings along her spine. She felt as if even their breathing had become part of each other. That without his mouth and body pressed against hers, she would wither and die in some strange never-known way.

As if she was in a dream, she felt the buttons at the back of her blouse give way under his fingers, shivering as he caressed her bared flesh, his hands lingering over her shoulders and the base of her throat as he eased the soft silk away.

She clung to him still, trembling at the sensations he was so knowingly arousing, yet wanting him to go on touching her. With a sound that was half a sigh, half a groan he lifted his mouth from hers and stared down into her flushed face. He raised his hand and gently traced the lines of her jaw to the pulse in her throat, then followed the slender line of her neck to the vulnerable hollows at its base. And paused.

Catriona glanced down and saw his fingers curving round the silver chain that held Jeremy's ring.

Their eyes met, his puzzled and with the first stirring of anger in their depths.

'You can't still be hoping,' he began. 'Not even you with that incredible optimism of yours . . .'

She tore herself out of his arms, her hand closing protectively over the ring.

'I suppose to—a man of the world like you'—she made the phrase sound like an insult—'a word like fidelity or loyalty has little meaning.'

'Applied to Jeremy, they're practically meaningless,' he said slowly. 'Applied to yourself . . .' He looked her over and his lips curled sardonically.

Crimson with anger as well as shame, she pulled her loosened blouse up over her shoulders. How could she have let him—*him* of all people behave like that? No one, not even Jeremy, had ever been permitted to kiss or touch her in that way. She had always had too much self-respect—Aunt Jessie had seen to that. Now she felt confused, as if her whole scale of values had been turned upside down by this witchcraft he had worked on her body.

Her eyes filled with tears, as she struggled vainly with her fastenings.

'Let me,' Jason spoke quietly.

'Don't touch me!' she breathed, her temper fighting for precedence over guilt and confusion. He bent his head and turned abruptly away, thrusting his hands into his pockets.

After a moment's hesitation, she pulled off the blouse altogether and snatched up the black sweater she had worn earlier, tugging it over her head with shaking hands. She could not look at him, and did not even want to know if he was looking at her. She still could not understand how she had come so near to betraying all her carefully held principles—and with a man like him. He must think that her feelings were as shallow as his own. He had a low opinion of women anyway and she was forced to admit that it would be difficult for anyone—even someone less cynical than himself

80

—to believe that she could still carry an aching heart for Jeremy and yet allow another man to make passionate love to her.

She was suddenly afraid she was going to burst into tears, and she sank down on the edge of the bed, covering her face with her hands. Her whole body was still in turmoil from his caresses and the treacherous physical weakness he had engendered was also affecting her emotions.

'Catriona,' he came and squatted in front of her, 'if you won't look at me, at least listen.'

'You have nothing to say to me that I want to hear.' Her hands were pressed so tightly over her eyes that little scarlet flames seemed to be flickering inside her lids. 'And I hope I never have to set eyes on you again either!'

He gave an exasperated sigh. 'You can't forgive me for making you see the truth about Jeremy, you stubborn little fool. You must have your illusion to cling to despite all the evidence.'

'What do you know about truth?' Her voice trembled. 'At least what Jeremy and I felt for each other was fine and clean, not like . . .'

Jason swore suddenly and violently, gripping her hands and dragging them away from her face. Dazedly, she stared at him.

'Tonight,' he said, and his voice was too quiet, too controlled, 'tonight, I nearly became your lover—there on that carpet or here on this bed. It wouldn't have mattered much, and I know damned well it would have mattered even less to you, so don't start carrying on as if I was some despoiler of innocence. And no matter how you may delude yourself about your feeling for my errant nephew, under your well-brought-up exterior, my sweet, you are all woman, so stop punishing us both for something that didn't happen anyway.' He paused. 'Or are you punishing me because it didn't happen?'

Catriona wrenched her hand free and hit him hard across

the face, then stopped, appalled at what she had done and fearful that he might enact some reprisal. Jason got slowly to his feet and stood looking down at her, his eyes chips of glazing steel.

'Enjoy your punishment,' he said softly, and went from her. She heard the outer door close behind him and hugged her arms convulsively across her body, trying to suppress the long, deep shiver that ran through her.

The small hard shape of Jeremy's ring pressed into her flesh. He might belong to Helen now, but his ring was hers and if she could no longer regard it as a love token, then at least it would be a talisman to keep her safe.

But from whom? a sly inner voice seemed to be asking. From Jason Lord—or from herself? And to that Catriona could find no answer, either then or in the long night that followed.

She still felt listless as she made her way to her new job the following Monday morning. She and Sally had spent a quiet weekend shopping for groceries and cleaning the flat, and on Sunday they had taken sandwiches and had a picnic lunch in Hyde Park, followed by a drowsy evening playing desultory Scrabble and watching television.

In many ways Catriona blamed herself for what had happened with Jason. She acknowledged that she had wondered what it would be like to be in his arms. Well, now she knew, and much good the knowledge had done her. At least now she had proved to herself exactly what form his relationship with a woman took, she thought bitterly. He had said some hard things about Jeremy, but was he any better himself? At least Jeremy had never tried to seduce her. If a small voice inside her pointed out that that was because she had been on her guard against allowing any such situations to develop in the past, she ignored it. She told herself resolutely that it was just as well she had found out what Jason was before she got any silly ideas about him in her head, although she didn't allow herself to specify the exact form her 'silliness' might have taken.

The most hurtful part of it all was that no mention of the word 'love' had ever passed his lips. Catriona had always been led to believe that men with seduction on their minds always told a girl they loved her first. She supposed she should be grateful that Jason had enough respect for her intelligence not to try such a well-worn subterfuge with her, but all it made her feel was cold and empty.

She wondered about returning to Scotland, but what was there for her there? She had no home now, and no job, both of which were available to her here in London, even if peace of mind was not. It seemed as if one chapter of her life had closed, but as yet she had no idea what the future could hold for her apart from heartache.

Her rather sombre thoughts kept her occupied during the ride on the Underground and the short bus journey which took her to the wide tree-lined road where the house belonging to the Trust was situated. Catriona was glad in a way that she had decided to take this job instead of plunging into the hurly-burly of a big general office where her heart-sore condition might have been more obvious and she might have become the object of unwanted speculation by the other girls.

In spite of her emotional dejection, Catriona could not help enjoying the feel of the sun on her face as she walked along or even feeling vaguely gratified at the appreciative wolf whistles from a group of workmen busily renovating a house, as they caught sight of her slim figure in the grey pinafore dress and scarlet shirt.

When she arrived at the Trust, identifiable by a small shabby board nailed to one of the gate pillars, she was a few minutes early so she had time to look the building over before she went in. It was a large house, even from the front, and she could see it extended well into the grounds at the rear. There was a prevailing air of shabbiness, in spite of the obvious fact that someone had recently been busy with a paintbrush. Even her untrained eye could spot missing slates and chimney stacks that needed re-pointing. Catriona sighed, remembering what an uphill job it had been to keep Muir House sound and weatherproof, quite apart from in good decorative order. She went up the wide stone steps to the front door, which stood ajar and peeped into a large uncarpeted hall. Somewhere she could hear the murmur of voices and the rattle of cups and cutlery, but she could not identify which of the several doors that opened off the hall the noise was coming from.

To her left, a wide flight of stairs, also uncarpeted, led upwards to a long landing, while ahead of her a dark-seeming passage led to the back of the house.

Catriona hesitated, then called, 'Is anyone there?' a little tentatively.

'Hang on. I'm coming!' a man's voice called in reply. One of the doors on the left of the hall opened and a young man appeared. He was of medium height and stocky build, wearing paint-stained corduroy trousers and an ill-used dark green sweater. He carried a tea towel in one hand and had another tucked round his waist like an apron.

'You've caught us washing up, I'm afraid,' he said. 'Can I help you?'

'I'm Catriona Muir.' She fumbled in her shoulder bag and produced the card from the agency.

He smiled delightedly at her. 'That's great. To be honest, I wondered whether—but never mind. Come on in.'

He crossed the hall and flung open the door opposite, ushering Catriona into a large sunny room that looked as if it had been recently hit by an earthquake. The main furniture was two massive old-fashioned dining room tables which had been extended to their fullest limits. One of them carried an equally old-fashioned-looking black typewriter. There were files everywhere, especially upside down on the floor, Catriona noted with a feeling of resignation, and more files protruded untidily from the open drawers of two big wooden filing cabinets. A white cupboard, used to store stationery, also stood open and in turmoil.

Catriona turned to look at her companion. His lips quirked ruefully. 'I'm not very well organised, I'm afraid,' he said with devastating understatement. 'I'm Andrew Milner, and if you want to just walk out of here and forget about it, I shall quite understand.'

Catriona managed a faint smile. 'Oh, I don't think I'm likely to do that.'

'The typewriter came out of the Ark, I think,' he went on rather sadly. 'And we haven't a photo-copier, just an old duplicator that spits ink at you when you least expect it.' He looked doubtfully at her clothes.

'Well—perhaps there's an overall somewhere, if I have to use the thing,' Catriona suggested.

'Yes, of course. I'm sure Jean would . . . well, you'll be meeting her shortly anyway. You must think I'm mad telling you all this, but the truth is that your predecessor had very different views of what an office should be like. She stuck it for three days, which I suppose was good of her under the circumstances, but there were—problems.'

'Well, I've got something to tell you, Mr Milner.' Catriona began to jut her chin, then decided it wasn't necessary after all. 'I've only ever worked as a secretary before for my aunt back in Scotland, so I may not live up to your requirements.'

His smile was cheerful and not diffident at all. 'Oh, but I think you will,' he said. 'In fact, I think I'd prefer someone who isn't just filling in time between executives.'

Catriona smiled too and put her handbag down on the table. 'Where would you like me to start?'

'Well, first of all—it's Andrew, please, not Mr Milner. And I hope you don't mind being Catriona. We try and cultivate a pretty informal atmosphere at the Trust—all part of the work we're doing. And the next thing is probably

85

this.' He dived into the stationery cupboard and emerged holding a jar of coffee and a bag of sugar. 'There's a gas ring over there and the kettle is full,' he told her. 'I'll go and get the milk.'

Over steaming mugs of coffee, he told her more about the work of the Trust itself and how it had been originally set up.

'James Henderson was a tremendous character, very down-to-earth and humorous, but full of compassion as well. He knew exactly what he wanted for this place, but unfortunately he died before it really got off the ground,' Andrew said regretfully. 'The Trust is now administered by his widow, Mrs Alice Henderson. I daresay you'll be meeting her soon.' The note of constraint in his voice was not lost on Catriona.

'Who uses the centre?' she asked as they left on a tour of the building. Andrew shrugged.

'Almost anyone needing a shelter of some kind. Homeless families, unmarried mothers, battered wives, teenagers who have left home for some reason, husbands or wives who have done the same. Sometimes we find out why, often we don't.' He gave her that warm smile again. 'And if they don't volunteer, we don't pry.'

He hesitated, then went on, 'There's a social work side to it, but I'm not pushing that at the moment. Soon, I hope to start building up case histories and try to do some sort of study to find what kind of pressures make people break loose. But I had to wait until I could get someone in the office that I could trust, and that the residents could also trust. Some of them are here for quite some time and continually changing faces in the office make them wary. Jean who looks after the housekeeping side and myself have been here since the centre opened.'

As they toured the building, Catriona could not help noticing the dilapidated state of many of the rooms and their furnishings.

'I suppose money is always a problem?' she asked shyly, not wishing to seem too critical of something she had not fully come to grips with.

'We're more fortunate than many organisations because we have a regular income of our own. Mr Henderson made over a massive part of his personal fortune and investments to finance the Trust.' They were standing by a window looking into a big untidy back garden with an overgrown lawn. Andrew sighed. 'You're going to work here, Catriona, so you might as well know. Inflation has hit our income pretty hard. In fact there were hints that we might have to do without help in the office, which is why, in a way, I was surprised when you actually materialised.'

He smiled ruefully. 'But there will have to be cuts in other ways, and this I'm afraid will mean goodbye yet again to all sorts of alterations and improvements I'd hoped for, although it's true to say I might not have got them anyway.'

'But if the money was there . . .' Catriona was puzzled.

Andrew gave her a straight look. 'It's Mrs Henderson,' he said quietly. 'She doesn't really approve of the centre and never has. She's quite open about it—believes Heaven helps those who help themselves. And she doesn't agree with the rather *ad hoc* way we run things here. She calls the residents inmates—not to their faces, I hasten to add—and feels I should summon them for morning prayer and grace before meals.'

'But that isn't your province, surely.'

'In a way I suppose it is, from her point of view.' He dragged aside the collar of his sweater, revealing the clerical collar beneath. 'I hope it doesn't put you off.'

'Not in the slightest, although you're not like any minister I've ever met,' Catriona laughed.

He quirked an eyebrow at her. 'I'll take that as a compliment, perhaps. Now come and meet Jean. There'll be a fair crowd in the kitchen part of the house and they'll eye you a bit at first. But don't try and push things and they'll soon

87

treat you as part of the furniture.'

Catriona did find the sudden silence that greeted her entrance with Andrew rather unnerving. She was not used to being the cynosure of so many eyes, but Jean's pleasant smile as she turned from the cooker where large pots of an appetising-looking stew were simmering, soon compensated. She was a slightly plump girl, in the way that good cooks often are, with softly curling brown hair, and Catriona took to her at once.

It was soon arranged that Catriona should share the midday meal at the centre in return for lending a hand with the serving and clearing away.

'I'm afraid you get roped in for everything in this place,' Jean said apologetically. 'Have you had any nursery school experience, by any chance?'

'Sorry, no,' Catriona laughed. 'Have you a lot of young ones in just now?'

'Yes, but it may not last. Things can change quite rapidly in a matter of days as people readjust and move on.' Jean's tone was placid and Catriona thought she was probably an ideal person to be in charge of such a fluid set-up as this appeared.

Later, as she helped Jean set places at the long trestle tables in the rather bare dining room, she asked for some help in identifying the current crop of residents.

'I could tell you their names, but I doubt if you'd remember. They'll start approaching you themselves in a day or two and you'll probably get the story of their lives along with their names—except for Mitch, that is.'

Catriona's interest sharpened. 'Who's Mitch?'

Jean laid a knife and fork rather precisely on the plastic table covering before replying. 'That's just it. Who is she? She behaves as if she has amnesia, but Andrew and I are not convinced. She doesn't show any of the genuine symptoms. She arrived in the middle of the night three weeks ago carrying a guitar in a case and that was all.'

'Does she play the guitar?'

'Not since she arrived, to my knowledge. If you go into the lounge you can't miss her. She sits in the corner cuddling the darned thing. One of the youngsters asked her to give them a tune soon after she arrived and she nearly attacked him. Andrew had to step in fast.'

'That's quite an unusual happening, then?'

'Violence? Yes, thank heaven. When you consider what a mixed bag of people we accommodate, it's a wonder that it doesn't happen more often. Usually people welcome some sort of contact, however superficial, with the other residents. But not Mitch. She's left severely alone now—and she shows no sign of wanting to stand on her own feet or move on. It's a bad sign, I'm afraid. We have had our tragedies in the past, but I don't want her to be one of them.'

Jean's voice was serious and Catriona waited in silence for a moment or two before asking, 'How do you know she's called Mitch?'

'We don't.' Jean lifted a tray of plastic beakers from a cupboard and began to set one at each place. 'She had a nightmare one night soon after she came here—woke everyone in her room screaming "Mitch, Mitch!" Wouldn't or couldn't explain, of course, so we decided to call her that for reference purposes.' She sighed. 'Andrew would like to put her in touch with Dr Winters, the psychiatrist at the General, but he doesn't feel there would be much point until we can make at least some sort of breakthrough with her ourselves. She totally rejects the idea of any kind of treatment at the moment, and we don't put pressure on anyone here—so checkmate.'

Catriona felt oddly curious about the enigmatic Mitch and was conscious of real disappointment when the girl failed to show up for the midday meal. After it was cleared away, she and Andrew began to make inroads on the chaos in the office and she was amazed to find how quickly the time passed.

She got home before Sally, who was rehearsing a new play for a lunchtime theatre club and had warned she might be late.

Catriona measured out spaghetti and assembled the ingredients for a bolognese sauce, before deciding that a bath and a shampoo were what she needed after her dusty afternoon. Half an hour later, she felt cleaner and at peace with the world as she sat on the hearthrug in her old red dressing gown, busying herself with hair-dryer and brush. When the doorbell sounded, she groaned a little. Sally was prone to forget her key when other considerations were paramount. She padded to the door and flung it wide, gazing with astonishment at the young man standing awkwardly outside.

'Hello, Catriona,' Jeremy said eventually. 'I can see I've called at a bad time. Can I come in?'

'I suppose so.' Catriona gave the belt of her robe a tightening tug and stepped aside reluctantly to allow him into the flat.

He glanced around. 'Sally not in?'

'I'm expecting her at any time.' Catriona was amazed to find how controlled her voice sounded in spite of the turmoil inside her. For weeks now she had longed for this moment, had hungered for the sight and sound of him, and now he was here.

He walked over to the fireplace and stood looking down at the rug. Catriona had forgotten how attractive he was and she stood, her arms folded tensely across her, watching him and remembering with fresh pain how happy they had been together.

With a sigh, he pulled a packet of cigarettes and a lighter from his pocket and offered them to her. She shook her head and he lit one for himself.

'Did—did you want something?' she asked diffidently, when he showed no sign of breaking the silence. He turned and looked at her, the usually laughing blue eyes dark with trouble.

'I shouldn't be here, Trina, and I know it, but I had to come. I've tried to keep away . . . I really have. I don't know what to say to you.'

'What is there to say?' Catriona asked wearily. 'It was my own fault, Jeremy. Women's magazines are full of advice to girls not to take holiday romances too seriously, and I did. You don't have to feel badly about it . . .' Her voice tailed away miserably.

'But I do.' He came over to her and stood looking down into her face. 'I wasn't just amusing myself. I loved you. I meant everything I said, and I wanted to marry you . . .'

'I don't think you should say any more,' Catriona interrupted him. She felt suddenly desperately uncomfortable. 'Don't forget you're engaged and . . .'

'Forget it!' He gave a short, mirthless laugh. 'I get little chance to do that. Helen's been staying with us and she and Mother have done nothing but talk about weddings and houses and furnishings until I could—break out.'

'Women like to talk of such things.' Catriona felt defensive about her own sex. 'I'd have thought that was what you would have wanted too.'

'Me?' He shook his head. 'I don't know what I want, Trina. I had it all worked out when I came back to London, but once I was back, everything started to—crumble somehow. All there seemed to be was work and more work, and when that eased off, Mother had Helen waiting.' He looked at her, his mouth wry. 'I see it now. Why couldn't I see it then?'

Catriona lifted a hand and pushed it wearily through her still-damp hair. 'I don't know what you want me to say,' she said unhappily. 'You've made your choice, after all.'

'I think I had it made for me,' he said quickly.

'Then you must be a fool.' Catriona spoke sharply and without weighing her words. 'It's a poor sort of man that lets his womenfolk decide his whole future rather than stand on his own feet . . .' She was shocked into silence by the

91

expression on Jeremy's face. She could see at once that she had hurt and offended him, and she realised with a pang that it was the first time that she had ever been openly critical of him. It occurred to her, too, judging by what Jason had once said, that open criticism by anyone of his actions had probably been lacking in Jeremy's life up to now.

'I thought you'd understand at least.' He sounded wounded.

'There's not a lot to understand,' she spoke more pacifically. 'You did ask Helen to marry you, after all, and people don't do that in this day and age unless they're in love. If you're having second thoughts now, they'll pass, I daresay.'

'I just don't know you like this.' His voice was genuinely perplexed.

'Perhaps I've had time to grow up a little since that summer in Torvaig.' She tried to sound gentle, but some of the hurt of betrayal came through the simplicity of her words.

'Is that what my dear uncle's been doing—helping you grow up?' he asked, and she winced at the unexpected spite in his tone. This was a side of Jeremy she had never seen before. She wanted to hit back at him, but she did not know what to say. He was nearer the target than he knew, she thought painfully.

'How did you come to meet him?'

'I was looking for you. Someone, your former landlady, gave me his address.'

'Oh—yes, I'd forgotten.' He looked at her frowningly. 'But I still don't understand . . . I mean, you're hardly Jason's type.'

'Hardly,' she said. Her throat felt constricted. 'But then I did think I was yours, and I was wrong about that too.'

He pitched his cigarette stub into an ash-tray and reached for her. 'Oh, Trina, my sweet!'

She stepped backwards, trying to avoid his encircling

arms in a kind of panic. 'Jeremy—no! It's not right, please!'

He didn't listen. 'Trina, ever since that night I've been thinking of you—of nothing else but you. Let me kiss you, sweetheart, please. I won't be able to bear it otherwise.'

Even as his lips touched hers, Catriona heard, with her heart sinking, the perennial cry of the spoiled child in his words. Oh, what was the matter with her? She was in Jeremy's arms, his passionate kisses were raining on her face. She should have been in the seventh heaven, and instead her predominating impulse was to pull herself free.

'What's the matter?' He stared down at her, his face flushed, puzzled by her lack of response.

'What about Helen? That's the matter,' Catriona said, but she was not even sure that was true any more.

'I'll think of something. Sweetheart, you must trust me.' He tried to take her in his arms again, but she evaded his embrace.

I did trust you, something inside her was screaming. Trusted you enough to leave everything I knew and come hundreds of miles to this concrete—prison of a city! Her hand crept to her mouth as if she had spoken the words aloud. She knew she had been unfair to her new home and that the changes in her life had certainly not been entirely for the worse. She thought of the centre and the challenges it presented, and of Jean and Andrew with whom she might become close friends. She thought of Sally's companionable gaiety. And then her mind closed down, refusing to yield to the next image which came unbidden and unwelcome, thrusting away the dark sardonic face of the man who had taught her in one brief lesson the meaning of response.

'I think you'd better go,' she told Jeremy, a slight betraying quiver creeping into her voice. 'Sally will be home any moment and . . .'

'I know.' Jeremy seemed mollified. 'Scottish propriety. You haven't changed as much as you think, sweetheart.'

He took her hand and pressed a kiss lingeringly into her

93

palm. '*Au revoir*,' he murmured. 'We'll meet again soon.'

When he had gone, Catriona sat down on the battered sofa and tried to assemble her thoughts into some kind of coherence. She had blamed Jeremy for being fickle, but was she, in fact, any better? Once, being in his arms had been her whole world. Now she was appalled at her own indifference to his caresses. I wanted him once, she thought bewilderedly, but did I even know what wanting was?

She could not believe what had happened to her in so short a time. She had thought her relationship with Jeremy had been a perfect thing. Now she was forced to recognise that its completeness had been a dream that could not withstand daylight's harsh reality.

She realised too that if things had been different, she might in all innocence have married Jeremy and lived a contented life, oblivious of the sharp sweet agony of physical passion as Jason had made her know it.

She buried her face in her hands, biting savagely at her lip, telling herself she would have been better off without that knowledge. Beyond that she refused to think.

And now, it seemed, whether she wanted or not, Jeremy was back in her life, and she was at a loss to know what to do about it. It would be wrong, she thought, to encourage him and perhaps cause him to break with Helen when she was so uncertain about the possibility of any future relationship between them. She would have to see Jeremy again, but on her terms this time, not his, and make this clear to him.

She got up rather drearily and went to the kitchen alcove to prepare the evening meal, telling herself that fatigue and hunger were what ailed her and all would seem better in the morning.

But as she sliced onions and tomatoes for the sauce, her thoughts were still elsewhere until a sharp pain across her thumb unpleasantly recalled her attention. Gingerly she ran the cold tap over the cut, wincing. This was another item to the account of the Lords, she thought stormily. It was an appropriate name for them—Lords of Creation as they no doubt thought themselves.

She threw the knife into the sink with a clatter.

'Damn them both,' she said tensely. 'I—I wish I'd never met them—either of them.'

But as she pressed her hand fiercely to her mouth, it was not her own blood but the warm, sensual pleasure of Jason's mouth that she seemed to taste.

CHAPTER FIVE

NEARING the end of her first week at the centre, Catriona felt a certain satisfied weariness. The office was now in apple-pie order, and she and Andrew had begun to rough out a scheme for detailing and filing the eventual case histories.

She had undergone her first battle with the baulky old duplicator and emerged slightly ahead and, which was best, she had begun to get to know some of the centre's residents.

Now, when she went into the kitchen or any of the other rooms they used, there were guardedly friendly greetings and one or two of the younger women asked her name and where she came from.

'That's a pretty name,' said Mrs Lamb, an exhausted-looking woman in her early thirties whose husband had left her penniless with three young children. 'I read a book called that once. At school it was,' she added hastily, as if apologising for any kind of superiority.

'I had a holiday in Scotland once, with Mum and Dad,' Linda chimed in. 'Smashing it was. Didn't half rain, though.'

Catriona looked at her with a slight pang, recalling that 'Mum and Dad' were both dead and that Linda, who had a small baby, was trying to cope as an unmarried mother and had recently been turned out of her room in a lodging house because the baby cried and annoyed the other tenants.

It was difficult, she thought, to do as Jean had advised her several times and remain as impersonal as she could. Jean and Andrew seemed to manage it so well—that sympathy without sentiment, kindness without patronage, yet they had both assured her that they were often full of uncertainties about the actual practical help they were being to the people who used the centre.

As she went back to the office, she noticed the door was standing open and she could hear voices. She peeped round the door and saw Andrew looking unnaturally neat and tidy in clerical collar and stock with a sports jacket instead of his usual disreputable sweater, standing rather defensively in front of his table.

'Oh, Catriona.' There was a faint note of relief in his voice as he greeted her. 'Mrs Henderson is here. Could you arrange for some coffee for her and . . .'

'No coffee for me, thank you.' Mrs Henderson, a thin, upright figure in an ice blue jersey suit, raised her hand. Her shrewd, rather chilly eyes studied Catriona. 'So this is the new secretary. She looks rather young. Is she capable?'

Catriona felt as if everything about her from the way she wore her hair to the length of her skirt had been assessed by the rather indomitable person confronting her. She was relieved to hear Andrew reply, 'Extremely,' in a rather dry tone.

'Well, that's a blessing. Come in, young woman. I presume you have work to do.' Mrs Henderson turned back to Andrew. 'I'm afraid I have some bad news for you, Mr Milner.' She delved into a capacious snakeskin handbag and produced a bulging envelope.

A special offer for readers of Mills & Boon

Four Mills & Boon Romances-FREE

We have chosen four Romances for you to enjoy FREE and without obligation as your special introduction to the Mills & Boon Reader Service.

Catriona, glancing at Andrew, saw his face stiffen as if he had just received a blow.

Mrs Henderson handed him the envelope. 'You'll get an official letter from the secretary to the Trust, of course, but I thought as I was in the neighbourhood I would let you know at once. The Trust cannot afford the sort of financial outlay this type of conversion would require.' She paused, and said in a slightly gentler tone, 'I am really sorry, Mr Milner. I know your heart was set on this, but in the present economic climate . . .' She sighed and shook her head.

Catriona, stricken, knew what Andrew must be feeling. He had obtained a number of estimates for converting the entire top floor of the centre which was at present unused and a maze of small attic rooms of varying shapes into flat-lets where homeless families could be accommodated to-gether, instead of being split up into separate male and female sleeping units as they had to be at present. Andrew felt strongly that it was degrading for husbands and wives to be separated in this way, and one of Catriona's earliest tasks had been to type a long and reasoned report support-ing the conversion scheme for the Trustees.

She bit her lip, knowing what high hopes he had had that the plan might be adopted.

There was a long silence, eventually broken by Mrs Henderson.

'We don't always see eye to eye, Mr Milner,' she said. 'I've never made any secret of the fact that I'm not totally in favour of the centre and its purpose, but I intend to do my best for it for my late husband's sake. The trouble is that the sum of money set aside originally for the Trust, though perfectly adequate at the time, has been eaten away by in-flation. The situation is extremely disturbing, and I think the time has come when we must look round for some alter-native means of financing the centre if it is to continue in its present form. Perhaps you would give the matter some thought. Otherwise . . .' She gave a deep sigh and shook her head slightly. 'Well, I must be going. I'm already late for my next appointment. Goodbye, Mr Milner. Goodbye, young woman.'

From the window, they saw her walk down the path to the car where the driver was waiting to help her in. The door slammed, the engine started and she was gone.

'Short and sweet.' Andrew's voice was ironic, a defence to conceal his true feelings, Catriona thought. 'Well, she turned our coffee down, but I think I could do with a cup.'

'I'll see to it,' she said immediately.

In the kitchen, Jean greeted her with a troubled smile.

'Was that Mrs Henderson's car just now? That usually means trouble.'

'I'm afraid it does,' Catriona sighed. 'Andrew got the thumbs down over the attic conversion.'

'Oh, no!' Jean stared at her. 'But it's so badly needed.'

'I know, but there simply isn't the money.' Catriona paused. 'Mrs Henderson was dropping hints too—about the future of the centre. She seems to feel it's uncertain without outside funds. Is there any way of getting more money—apart from the Trust, I mean?'

'Who knows?' Jean sat down at the kitchen table, her shoulders drooping defeatedly. 'We've certainly never had any luck in the past. Andrew has constantly applied to other charitable foundations, but the answer has always been that they're fully stretched themselves.' She sighed. 'The begging letters go out, but very little cash comes in. The main trouble in the past has been that Mrs Henderson would never allow any fund-raising to go on. She's always been—well, dog-in-the-manger about permitting help from outsiders. This was her late husband's pet project and it had to remain firmly under the wing of the Henderson Trust, so now in many ways I feel we've missed the boat.'

'I feel sure she's changed her mind now,' Catriona said slowly.

'Oh, I'm sure too,' Jean said drily. 'But is it in time to save the centre? It's so dreadful to think that Andrew's worked all this time maybe for nothing. He's tried so hard and all he's had in return are disappointments and rejections—and from people who are supposed to be on his side,' she concluded with a fierceness that surprised Catriona.

'I'm sure it's not too late,' she said. 'Perhaps we can launch an appeal . . . do something at least.'

'Hmm.' Jean sounded unconvinced. 'But we're not one of the big fashionable charities, Catriona, that can afford to spend money to get money. We haven't funds to splash out on the sort of publicity we'd need. Besides, we'd be like the Babes in the Wood in that sort of set-up. All we really know about is looking after people.'

'But there are often charity appeals on television,' Catriona began, but Jean cut in.

'I daresay, but I don't think our appeal is wide enough for that sort of coverage. Anyway, who do we know in the television world?' She got up. 'Was it the milk you came for? I'll take it if you like.' She gave Catriona a forced version of her usual sunny smile and went out of the kitchen.

Catriona remained at the table, lost in thought. She had plenty to occupy her mind. Firstly, from the way Jean had spoken it was obvious that her feeling for Andrew went far deeper than merely that of one colleague for another. She wondered if Andrew was aware of the fact and hoped very much that he was. Even on a relatively brief acquaintance she was sure they would be ideally suited to each other, and she hoped everything would work out for them. But, on the face of it, things did not look too hopeful. They were probably the type of couple who needed time to let their feelings grow and develop, and their relationship might well be affected if there was increasing worry over the future of the centre or if it, in fact, were to close down.

Catriona sighed and got up, intending to return to the

office and get on with her interrupted work, but the realisation that Jean would be there with Andrew gave her pause. That could be a situation where three would most definitely be a crowd, she decided wryly. Instead, she wandered into the big communal sitting room, usually empty at this time of the day, and went over to one of the long windows. She needed time to think, to try and come to terms with the idea that had forced itself into her reluctant brain, prompted by one of Jean's parting remarks. She caught sight of a movement out of the corner of her eye and, turning, realised the room wasn't deserted after all. The girl Mitch, her guitar clutched defensively across her, was sitting on a low stool in the corner. Catriona had seen her a number of times during her week at the centre and had always spoken to her without receiving the slightest of responses. For a moment she was tempted to ignore her and have her think in peace, but she knew it would be wrong to waste an opportunity to try and get through to the girl.

'I play the guitar,' she remarked casually. 'And I sing. Do you sing, Mitch?' She glanced across and was rewarded by the slightest shake of the head. 'That's a pity,' she went on, 'because that's a lovely guitar. It must have cost a lot of money. Have you had it long?'

Again, after a long pause, that infinitesimal shake of the head.

Catriona tried again. 'What's your favourite tune? I've got several.'

She began to reel off names of well-known folk songs, but Mitch's face was unresponsive.

'Do you know this one?' Catriona tried her with the refrain of the *Skye Boat Song*. 'Or maybe this?' On an impulse she switched to a particular favourite of hers, the plaintive swing of the *Eriskay Love Lilt*, humming the chorus until she got to the last phrase, 'Sad am I without thee', which she sang in her warm, clear soprano. And this time there was a response.

Mitch leapt to her feet, the stool crashing to the ground. She still cradled her guitar in her arms, but her eyes blazed.

'Leave me alone, can't you?' Her voice rose almost hysterically to a shriek and she rushed out of the room. Catriona stared after her, bewildered by the reaction. It wasn't what she had hoped for, she thought unhappily, but at least it was a beginning—of sorts.

She was still depressed when she got back to the flat that night, and Sally lent her a sympathetic ear.

'What you need,' she announced at the end of the recital of the day's woes, 'is taking out of yourself. How would you like to go to a party?'

'A party?' Catriona perked up a little. 'Whose?'

'Now for the bad news—Moira's. She's having some people round to her flat tomorrow night and she's invited me for some obscure reason. And I was told I could "bring my little Highland flatmate" along.' She grinned at Catriona's instant grimace. 'Yes, I know, but Moira's parties are generally regarded as fun and you might surprise yourself and enjoy it. You've been looking like Marley's ghost for days.'

Catriona shook her head hesitantly. 'I—I've nothing to wear.'

'Liar,' Sally said roundly. 'What about that Ondine thing you've got hidden in a box on the wardrobe?'

'It can stay there.' Catriona was conscious of a sudden tight sensation in her throat. 'I—I don't want to wear that again.'

There was a brief silence while Sally studied her, and then she said triumphantly, 'Of course—you can wear the Mistake.'

'Thanks a lot!' Catriona was amused, but Sally waved a hand at her impatiently.

'Mistake for me, but on you it could be sensational,' she said, uncurling herself from the settee and vanishing into the bedroom. Her voice came floating back. 'I bought it for an audition because it suited the role I was trying for. Madness, really, because they both couldn't have been more wrong for me. I didn't get the part and I was stuck with the dress. Sheer disaster, darling, from beginning to end.'

She returned with a drift of filmy whiteness over one arm. 'Try it on,' she urged, and Catriona complied, a little reluctantly. But once the zip was fastened and the soft folds of the incredibly full skirt twitched into place, Catriona was forced to admit that Sally could be right. It was a dress for dreaming in, all innocence and demureness. The sweeping neckline barely acknowledged her shoulders and only hinted at the rounded softness of her breasts. The wide, semi-transparent sleeves belled to the wrists where they were captured into a narrow ruffle. Anything less suitable for Sally's lively directness would have been hard to envisage.

She thought almost idly, 'I look like a bride.' But it was not a happy thought and looking in the mirror at her shadowed eyes and mouth grown wistful, she hated her own vulnerability.

At her shoulder, Sally said gently, 'You don't have to go, you know.'

Catriona's chin lifted with some of her old defiance.

'I'll go,' she said. 'And I'll wear the dress, if I may. It's beautiful.'

As she hung the dress back in the wardrobe, her hands were shaking. She had no doubt at all that Jason Lord would be at Moira's party. All she had to do was seek him out and ask him to help her to get an appeal for the centre on television. He had so many contacts in the media, he would surely know how to help. She told herself this over and over again, trying to convince herself, to bolster up her confidence when every instinct she possessed shrank from such a course of action. She couldn't pretend he would have forgotten their last encounter and its stormy ending.

And yet here she was approaching him yet again. It would

serve her right, she told herself, if she met with total rejection. But at the same time, she knew she had to go through with it for the centre's sake. Even if she met with a downright refusal, at least she would know that she had tried.

But when she and Sally finally stood in Moira's cramped hall, all her uncertainties allied to overwhelming shyness came back to plague her.

'Hell!' Sally looked at her watch. 'We're nearly half an hour late and we're still the first to arrive. What's the betting Moira's not even dressed yet?'

The young Filipino girl who had admitted them took their wraps and asked them in charmingly accented English to wait in the living room.

Catriona gasped when she looked around her. Walls and carpet were a stark white. Everything else—upholstery and drapes—was a rich glowing red. Sally sighed.

'Only Moira would dare with hair that colour,' she said.

Catriona nodded slowly. The room was spectacular but in spite of its colour, curiously unwelcoming. But at the same time she felt a sense of relief that she and her pale dress could sink into obscurity against the walls if she wished.

Moira, when she appeared, was no less spectacular than her background. She had chosen a tight sheath of a dress, the starkness of its predominating black relieved by narrow golden stripes. It fitted her voluptuous body as if she had been sewn into it and the deep plunge of the neckline left little to the imagination. Her scent, sensuous and musky, seemed to fill the room as she entered, her hips swinging provocatively beneath the revealing lines of her gown.

'Darlings!' A smile which never reached her eyes embraced them both. Without uttering another word, she appraised their dresses and dismissed them before sauntering to the enormous hi-fi unit which almost filled one wall and switching on something low-keyed and Latin-American with an insidious sophisticated rhythm.

'And that's just the rehearsal. Imagine the performance!' Sally murmured under its cover.

Catriona ducked her head to hide her smile as Moira's voice, insinuatingly sweet, reached them.

'Actually, you could be angels and help me. Poor Jasmine hasn't had much experience with parties and she staged rather a drama over the canapés earlier. If you would just pop into the kitchen and see that all is well, I'd be eternally grateful.'

There was a stunned silence. Glancing at Sally, Catriona saw angry flags of colour flying in her cheeks, but when she spoke her voice and smile were as sweet as Moira's.

'Of course we don't mind. And if you found us some aprons, we could always hand drinks round as well.'

It was Moira's turn to redden. 'I think that's going a little too far,' she said coldly, and returned to her task of selecting records from the crowded shelves of the unit.

'I knew there was an ulterior motive behind that invitation,' Sally muttered when they were in the kitchen, surveying the trays of mouthwatering delicacies that had been set out there. 'She just wanted some extra unhired help for the evening. I'm sorry to have got you into this, love. I thought you'd enjoy a showbiz party.'

'And so I shall—as it's my first and probably my last.' Catriona gave a reluctant grin. 'I don't think Moira will forgive either of us in a hurry for that crack of yours about aprons!'

In many ways it turned out to be quite fun, putting finishing touches to the buffet, as Jasmine was soon kept busy running backwards and forwards to let people in and seemed pathetically grateful for their help. The girls gathered that Moira's contribution to the proceedings had been to spend the afternoon on her bed, giving contradictory orders through her face pack, and that Jasmine who had been with her for two weeks was now looking for another job.

By the time they returned to the living room, the party was in full swing and Catriona hung back a little, beset with another bout of shyness. The room seemed incredibly crowded. A space in the middle had been cleared for dancing, and a number of couples were already swaying to the soft sinuous rhythms coming from the hi-fi. Catriona found herself a glass of fruit juice and stood quietly in a corner, amusing herself by trying to match names to some of the more recognisable faces, but the face she was really searching for was not there.

Catriona felt her heart sink. The only reason she had come to the party was to see Jason. She had rehearsed in her mind almost a hundred times what she was going to say to him, how she was going to present the centre's case in such a way that he could not refuse to help. And it was only nervousness at the possibility of his refusal, she told herself resolutely, that was making her heart pound in this oddly fierce way and her body feel cold and clammy in spite of the heat of the room.

She knew she was being a fool to pin so much hope to this idea. A fool to think he would even listen to her—after the other evening. But those memories were taboo, she tried to remind herself, as that aching languor crept into her limbs again at the thought of his body against hers. She must forget all about that, as he undoubtedly would. No man, especially one like Jason Lord, would want to remember that he had been rejected by an unsophisticated girl, she thought painfully. And why should he care, when there were always women like Moira to give him everything he demanded? Women who were not always conscious that their background and upbringing totally renounced the kind of permissive relationships that seemed an acceptable part of Jason's world.

Catriona had never had any difficulty in assimilating the strict pre-marital morality of the community round Torvaig, but, as she was forced to acknowledge to herself, this might have been because no serious temptations had ever presented themselves. Aunt Jessie's strictures on the respect a man should have for an unmarried girl had melted into oblivion under Jason's lips and hands. And if he had aroused cravings in her flesh that only he could satisfy—well, that was something she would have to try and live with. For the moment, the centre and the people who depended on its continuation were all-important, and her pride and emotions would have to take second place.

Sally appeared at her side. 'Circulate,' she hissed, 'or Moira will have you back in the kitchen washing glasses!'

Catriona chuckled and was just going to accompany Sally to meet some of the theatre club actors she was working with, when she was suddenly aware of a new arrival. Jeremy, on his own, was standing just inside the door looking round. Before Catriona could look away or lose herself in the laughing group already closing round Sally, he had seen her. She groaned inwardly. He was the last person she had expected to see. She had forgotten that his fiancée was related to Moira Dane.

'Trina.' He reached her side and stood smiling down at her. 'What a surprise!'

'I was just thinking the same,' she tried to sound non-committal. 'Er—where's Helen tonight?'

'Oh, she had to go north unexpectedly. Her grandmother is ill or something.'

'Didn't she want you to go with her?' Catriona looked at him curiously.

'Out of the question, I'm afraid,' he said airily. 'Far too much on at work. But I was at a loose end tonight, so I decided to take advantage of Moira's invitation.' He gave her the smile that had once had the power to charm the heart from her body. 'But how come you're here, Trina? I didn't know you and Moira were friends.'

Catriona shrugged. 'I was invited along to make up numbers with Sally, I suppose,' she answered awkwardly.

He smiled again and took her hand. 'Things couldn't have worked out better, could they?' he said softly. 'Come and dance with me.'

Catriona hesitated, intensely conscious of Moira's speculative gaze fixed on them from across the room. Quite apart from her own lack of inclination, she could imagine Jason Lord's reaction if he was to arrive and find her with Jeremy.

'Come on,' Jeremy urged impatiently, and with an inward sigh, she accompanied him to join the other dancers. The last thing she wanted was any kind of scene. The tempo of the music was slower now, and Jeremy pulled her close, resting his cheek against her hair.

'Happy?' he murmured after a moment or two had elapsed.

She was at a loss to know what to answer. To be truthful, she felt on edge and uncomfortable—emotions she had never expected to experience in Jeremy's embrace. But it did not seem an appropriate time to tell him, so she gave a little unintelligible murmur. Her discomfort increased as he put his lips against her forehead.

'Jeremy!' she protested, holding herself away from him.

'What's wrong?' He seemed genuinely puzzled.

'You—you wouldn't do that if Helen was here.'

'Maybe not, but she's away.'

'And that makes some sort of difference?'

He shrugged. 'Helen's a big girl now. She knows what the score is.' He tried to draw her close again, but she determinedly held him away. 'Oh, for heaven's sake, Trina, relax!'

'Moira is watching us,' she warned wretchedly.

'Let her.' His grin was suddenly malicious. 'She'd rather see you with me than with dear Uncle Jason, anyway.'

Catriona absorbed his words with an odd pang. It occurred to her that she had been doing her best to ignore the fact that Jason and Moira were more than friends, and she did not care to inquire too closely into her reasons. She did

107

not feel capable of analysing her feelings, or the recent changes that seemed to have recently overtaken some of her most cherished beliefs. She had talked glibly of fidelity to Jason, but did she really know what the word meant? And what had she been faithful to? A summer dream that had played her false. She had given her heart to a smiling stranger who had promptly repaid her by betraying her with another girl, and was now apparently quite prepared to reverse the situation by betraying his fiancée in turn.

What a fool I've been, she thought with a fleeting pang of regret for that lost summer and its innocence. She was thankful when the music stopped and she had an excuse to escape. After that she was almost constantly occupied dancing with the actors in the group gathered around Sally, and she was beginning to forget the confused state of her emotions in frank enjoyment of the party, when Moira's sudden squeal, 'Darling!' told her what a fleeting look confirmed—that Jason Lord had arrived at last. It cost a lot to look away again, and try to pretend that Moira was not in his arms, her body pressed seductively against his with her red mouth already lifted for his kiss. Instead she managed to smile up at tall, bearded Ian who was soon to start work with the Royal Shakespeare Company and went on chatting just as if all her thoughts and senses were not suddenly concentrated painfully elsewhere.

When finally their eyes did meet as he stood at the improvised bar, the centre of a laughing group, she saw him pause fractionally as he lit a cheroot, registering her presence with slightly raised eyebrows. He didn't look angry or resentful to see her, Catriona thought thankfully. Perhaps she would be able to approach him during the course of the evening, after all, without too much awkwardness.

With a suddenly lightened heart, she began to hum the tune that she and Ian were dancing to, adding the words too as they came back to her. It was only when she noticed Ian's broad grin, and the approving smiles from the couples around them, that she realised that her vocal accompaniment had been louder than she had intended. Blushing, she relapsed into silence, only to encounter immediate and voluble protests from all sides, to her horrified embarrassment.

'Don't stop, sweetie. That was charming.' A tall, blonde woman took her arm and propelled her across the room towards Moira. 'Now then, darling. You didn't tell us we had a new talent among us tonight.'

Catriona prayed that the floor would open and swallow her, but it remained inimically solid. Moira was smiling, but the look in her eyes was glacial.

'Frankly, I had no idea myself,' she said lightly. 'But as opportunity seems to have knocked for Miss—er—Muir, I suppose we can't deny her a public performance.'

'Oh, no, I couldn't,' Catriona broke in miserably.

'But you obviously can.' Moira looked and sounded bored. 'Robbie there will accompany you. He can play anything.'

To her consternation, Catriona saw that the plump, bespectacled figure of Robbie was already opening the baby grand piano which stood at one end of the room.

'Tell me the song and the key, darling. I'll do the rest,' he said cheerfully as Catriona was ushered unwillingly to his side. 'You're the star turn. Can't let your audience down.'

She pressed her hands to her hot face. 'Well, do you know *I Know Where I'm Going?*'

He hummed a couple of bars, struck an experimental chord or two and nodded in satisfaction. 'Ready when you are.'

Catriona's flush died away and she was almost as white as her dress when she turned to face the crowded room, now politely hushed and waiting for her to sing. As Robbie began to play the introduction, she saw Moira sitting on the edge of the semi-circle that had formed. Jason was standing behind her and as Catriona watched, Moira turned to him murmuring something and he bent towards her, smiling, his eyes on Catriona. There was something in that smile—

something sardonic, even derisory—that made Catriona's hackles rise. So they were laughing at her—waiting for her to fail and make a fool of herself in front of all these people. Well, she would just show them! She lifted her chin and sang: 'I know where I'm going, And I know who's going with me. I know who I love, But the dear knows who I'll marry.'

The notes fell warm, pure and rounded into the expectant silence. She had chosen the song because it was simple and well known. Now, even as she sang, she realised how appropriate the words were for the situation in which she found herself, and the realisation lent her voice an added huskiness and depth. 'Some say he's black, But I say he's bonny . . .'

She could not look at him where he lounged, his arms folded indolently across the back of Moira's chair. Instead she fixed on other people—on Ian, on the blonde woman who had started it all, even on Jeremy who was fixing her with a burning gaze she would ordinarily have found an embarrassment—and sang to them, making them believe she sang for each one of them alone.

When she finished there was a moment's hush, then she was almost overwhelmed by the applause. People were calling for more, while Robbie sat and surveyed the keyboard with a small, satisfied smile. Catriona smiled and bowed and quietly but firmly refused to sing again. Moira did not join in the applause. She rose and waited for Catriona to approach her, her body taut in that gorgeous black and gold dress. Catriona thought with a sudden sense of detachment that she looked like a cross between a tigress and a queen wasp.

'Well done, darling. Any more party pieces you'd like to show us?' Moira's voice was light, then she turned and walked away in the direction of her bedroom.

'Take no notice.' It was Robbie, smiling and tossing a

110

significant wink at Moira's retreating back. 'Only room for one star around here, you know.'

Before Catriona could reply, she was surrounded by a small crowd of people wanting to congratulate her and asking if she sang professionally. When at last she was able to tear herself away, her face felt stiff with smiling and her throat ached from saying, 'Thank you.' She went into the empty kitchen and poured herself a glass of water, watching the mist form and clear on the tumbler.

'So there you are,' Jeremy said from the doorway. He walked forward, smiling at her. 'My Trina. I once told you you'd be a sensation. Remember?'

'Yes,' she said, still conscious of that curious sense of detachment.

'And that song—it was always my favourite. You remembered that too.' His breath smelt of whisky as he leaned towards her.

'No,' she said. 'I'd forgotten that.'

'Trina,' his voice was reproachful, 'don't tease me. You know how I feel about you.'

'I'm beginning to, I think.' She looked at him, studying the good-looking features which soon would begin to blur with good living and self-indulgence. 'You want the best of both worlds—a rich wife and a girl-friend on the side. Well, that's not what I want, Jeremy.'

'What do you want, then?' he demanded sullenly. 'Me to finish with Helen, I suppose. Well, perhaps I will, but these things take time. You can't expect . . .'

'No.' She shook her head gravely. 'I can't expect—and I don't.'

She lifted her hand to her throat and tugged at the silver chain. The fragile links snapped, and she took the chain and the ring it held and put them into his hand.

Jeremy looked down at them blandly. 'I don't understand.'

'Ah, but you will,' she said. 'You will.' She drank the rest of her water and put the tumbler down on the stainless steel draining board.

'You're upset,' he persisted. 'You've every reason to be, I admit. But I'll make it all up to you. Now Helen's away, we have a real chance to get to know each other all over again.'

'Poor Helen,' she said. 'But there'll be no need to cause her any heartache. You see, I do know you, Jeremy, and I know myself now better than I did, and things are better as they are, believe me.'

'Trina.' He caught her arm as she walked past him towards the door. 'We can't talk here. Let's go. Just you and me—the way it once was. We'll go back to your place and . . .'

'No,' she said. 'Please take your hand off my arm.'

'Now listen——' he began aggressively, and Jason said, 'No, *you* listen. She asked you to take your hand from her arm.' He was leaning against the doorframe, his face enigmatic.

Jeremy opened his mouth as if to speak, looked down sharply at the ring and broken chain he was still clutching, then swung round, brushing past Jason through the doorway. Jason stood back to let him pass and steadied the violently swinging door with his arm.

It was as if the dreamlike bubble enclosing Catriona had suddenly burst. She was back down to earth, face to face with the man who had every reason to feel resentment towards her and of whom somehow she had to ask a favour.

She cleared her throat nervously. 'I know what you must be thinking.'

'Then you must be extremely clever. I'm not even sure myself.' He walked past her to the refrigerator and pulled the door open. 'I'm not really spying on you, you see, or protecting you against my nephew's probably drunken advances. I just want some ice for my Scotch.' He opened the freezer compartment. 'Ah!'

112

'I need your help,' she said—too quickly, she knew, but he had put the ice in his glass and was on his way back to the party and she might never have the opportunity or the courage to ask him again if she failed now.

Jason looked at her, his mouth twisting sardonically. 'On the contrary. The events of the past half-hour seem to prove that you can manage perfectly well by yourself.'

'I don't mean that sort of help.' Her palms felt moist and she wiped them surreptitiously down her skirt. 'It—it's not for me really.'

'Then who is it for?' He held his glass up to the light, apparently admiring the cool amber of the liquid it contained. 'Male or female? Or am I being indiscreet?'

She looked at him, puzzled. His tone was light, but there was something behind the words that she could not pinpoint.

'Well—male, really, I suppose,' she said, thinking of Andrew. 'Though lots of other people are involved as well.'

'Who is he?'

How odd that he should ask her that, and not what help it was that she wanted, she thought bewilderedly. But at least he was listening to her, even if she did seem to have less than a hundred per cent of his attention. Nor was he taunting her about that other evening as she had half feared he might. In fact, it might never have happened—might all have been some figment of her imagination. He was like a stranger, half turned from her, his eyes fixed on the floor or on the glass in his hand, never on her. Yet once—then—he had looked at her as if he was etching the sight of her on some inner vision.

She shook herself back to the present, and began haltingly to tell him about the centre and its problems. He listened frowningly as she described the Trust and its shortcomings, and the difference that an influx of money would make to the work Andrew was trying to do there.

Only then did he interrupt. 'But what can I do? I'm not

a trustee, and I don't know anyone who is.'

Catriona shook her head, her cheeks flaming. 'I thought that you could—perhaps—get someone to do something for us—on television. An appeal, something like that. You know so many people . . .'

He gave a small explosive laugh. '*Television!*' he began as the kitchen door banged open under the impact of Moira's entrance.

'I see.' Her voice dripped acid. 'Hiding away with our little prima donna. What curious places you do choose for your assignations, Jason darling! Aren't you coming back to the party? We're all desolate without you.'

'Hush, my sweet.' Jason took a meditative sip from his glass. 'Miss Muir is appealing on behalf of her favourite charity.'

'How touching! You should have said something earlier, Miss Muir. We could have passed a hat round after your song.'

The words were an insult in themselves, but the tone in which they were uttered cut Catriona to the bone. She lifted her chin and attempted a brave imitation of her smile.

'What a pity I didn't think of it. I'll say goodnight now, Miss Dane. Thank you for inviting me to your party. It's been—quite an experience.'

As she walked past Moira to reach the door, the actress moved her arm slightly and some of the liquid in the glass she was holding splashed down the front of Catriona's white dress.

'Oh, no!' Catriona looked down at the soaking stains through a hot blur of tears. Everything was suddenly ruined —her plea to Jason and now this lovely dress. And she had humiliated herself for nothing. Jason's scathing remarks revealed plainly that he had neither forgiven nor forgotten, and the hurt that was filling her being was not entirely to do with injured pride.

114

She started blindly for the living room and started when his hand descended on her arm.

'I'll take you home,' he said.

'No!' she cried, trying to wrench herself free.

'Don't argue, and don't make a scene. You'd be out of your depth in this company,' he said. He was steering her quickly through the laughing, chattering groups, calling goodnight, responding to the sympathetic noises from some of the women when they saw the state of Catriona's dress. She went with him mechanically, waiting silently while he fetched her wrap, damming back the tears as they waited for the lift to take them down to ground level again.

They were in the car and driving back to the flat before Jason spoke.

'I'm sorry,' he said.

She shook her head. 'There's no need to be.'

'That crack about your charity appeal was unnecessary,' he said abruptly. 'It's the sort of language Moira understands. I forget that you're not in her league.' He glanced down at her. 'And I'm sorry about your dress too.'

'Well, that certainly wasn't your fault,' she said haltingly.

'No?' He smiled faintly.

'And it's not my dress. It's Sally's, and that's what makes it so—awful.' She could not quite suppress the sob in her voice.

'Young Sal won't blame you. She knows Moira too well,' he said.

She looked at him sideways under her lashes, puzzled at this rather edged reference to the woman he was supposed to be in love with. Perhaps when your face and body were as beautiful as Moira's, men did not mind so much about your character, she thought. It was unlikely any way that the kindness and consideration for the other person's feelings that Aunt Jessie had always laid stress upon would have any place in their sort of relationship. She swallowed painfully, hating the picture of them together that her imagination was creating.

When they arrived back at the flat, Jason parked in the street below and switched off the engine.

Catriona looked at him uncertainly. 'Thank you for bringing me home,' she said formally.

'Aren't you going to invite me in?'

Her uncertainty increased. 'I—I—do you want some coffee?'

'Not particularly. I thought you wanted to talk to me about the Henderson Trust and its problems.'

'I didn't think you were interested.'

'Don't sulk.' He reached out and tugged slightly at one silky strand of hair. 'I'm here and I'm ready to listen. Do I get invited in?'

'Yes,' she said, her heart pounding unevenly at the thought of being alone with him again.

Upstairs in the living room, he put a light to the gas fire and then walked across to the kitchen alcove and picked up the kettle.

'I'll cope with the coffee while you try and salvage Sal's dress,' Jason tossed at her over his shoulder.

When she emerged from the bedroom a few minutes later, wrapped from throat to ankle in her dressing gown, he was placing two steaming mugs on a tray and carrying them to the settee. He lifted an inquiring eyebrow at her.

'The label said washable, so I have it soaking in cold water. I'll just have to hope for the best,' she said. 'Please excuse the way I look.'

'But it didn't seem worth getting dressed again as you'll be going to bed soon anyway,' he finished for her, and laughed. 'Don't jump like that, Catriona, or you'll spill scalding coffee all over yourself.'

She knew she was blushing and sat down at the opposite end of the settee, as far away from him as she could get, swathing the folds of her dressing gown around her feet.

Jason leaned back, stretching his long legs to the fire and closing his eyes. The only source of light came from a small table lamp in the corner, and the shadowy room accentuated the planes and angles of his dark face in a disturbing manner.

Watching him, Catriona was assailed by a wave of longing so intense that it threatened to overwhelm her. Her eyes lingered over his face, coming to rest at last on the firm, aggressive lines of his mouth. The memory of that mouth and the sensations it could evoke brought a tremulousness to her own lips and a softness to her eyes. She had never known what it was to want a man before. Her aunt had always hinted that it was only men who had needs and desires to be assuaged, but Catriona knew now that this was far from the truth.

'I thought you wanted to talk.' His voice held lazy amusement and with a shock of embarrassment she realised he was quite aware of her regard.

'What more can I tell you?'

'All the facts. I have a feeling that you've been holding out on me. So far I've gathered that money exists to finance this—altruistic venture. All well and good. So why isn't it doing so?'

'There simply isn't enough any more,' she said lamely.

'Is that the real reason—or is cash being deliberately withheld, perhaps because the Trust feel there is some sort of wastage or mismanagement going on?'

'Certainly not!' Catriona spoke indignantly. 'Mrs Henderson may not approve of the work at the centre, but she wouldn't stoop to anything like that.'

'Ah,' he murmured, reaching for his coffee. 'So Mrs Henderson doesn't approve? Then why doesn't she have the Trust wound up? That seems the obvious procedure.'

'Because she would be betraying her late husband's wishes,' Catriona said stiffly. 'And that's part of the trouble. Mr Henderson thought the money he had left in trust would be enough, without applying to outside sources. He just didn't visualise what inflation was going to do.'

'Epitaph for a philanthropist,' Jason said shortly. 'So what you're all really attempting is a rescue at the eleventh hour from the fruits of improvidence.'

Catriona looked at him defiantly. 'You could put it like that.'

'I could put it more strongly still,' he returned. 'Surely this fellow—Milner—who runs the place could see the way things were going?'

'Andrew has other things to think about, apart from money,' Catriona defended him.

'Lucky Andrew. Tell me, does he know you're asking me for help like this?'

'Oh, no,' she said quickly. 'It was all my own idea. I—I didn't say anything deliberately in case you refused. But you will help—won't you?'

He swallowed the rest of his coffee and put the cup down on the table. 'I'm sorry, Catriona, I left the magic wand in another suit.' He saw her bite her lip and lifted his hand resignedly. 'I'm sorry—that was flip, I know, but it's also true. There is no instant solution to this sort of problem. All I can promise is that I'll think it over and have a word with a few people who may have ideas of their own.' He gave her a considering look. 'But I think any kind of direct appeal is out. What we come up with may not be entirely acceptable. Have you thought of that?'

'All that matters is that it should work,' she said almost fiercely.

'So the end justifies the means. That's a ruthless point of view coming from you,' he said, smiling faintly. 'Does it mean so much to you, then?'

She thought of silent, unhappy Mitch nursing her guitar with empty eyes, and Linda with her baby and all the other people for whom the centre was perhaps the only refuge in a hostile world.

'Yes,' she said simply. 'It means a lot.'

She thought she heard him sigh, but she must have been mistaken because when she looked at him he was smiling again, but that unpleasant, sardonic smile that always disturbed her.

'And in return?' he asked softly.

'I—I don't understand.' She shook her head slightly so that her hair swung like a silken veil between them.

'I thought you were the girl who didn't like to be under an obligation.' He got up. In the half-light, he seemed taller than ever. 'Yet, if I do come up with something, you'll be deeper in debt to me than ever. And a day's housework will hardly cover it this time—so what did you have in mind?'

Catriona swallowed. The room seemed so quiet suddenly that she thought she could hear the sound of her own tumultuous heartbeats. Why was she hesitating? Every nerve, every pulse in her body was telling her that she wanted him. And yet not like this—a casual encounter, something seemed to cry inside her, prompted by a brief transitory desire on his side, and supposed gratitude on hers. But perhaps this was all there was for her. She might want more, but she was still sane enough to recognise that she could be crying for the moon.

'Well?' he prompted quietly.

She rose slowly to her feet, automatically tightening the belt of her housecoat with fingers that shook. He stood, his hands resting lightly on his hips, watching her walk towards him, but he made no attempt to touch her, even when she was barely inches away from him.

She paused uncertainly, looking up into his face, trying to read his enigmatic expression.

'I—I'll do anything you want,' she said huskily.

He reached out and lifted the heavy fall of hair back from her face, letting his hand stroke her throat and the delicate line of her jaw.

'Convince me,' he whispered.

Mutely, she lifted her face and he bent to her, touching

119

her mouth with his in a kiss that was as light as a drifting leaf. His hand moved under her hair, clasping the nape of her neck, pulling her towards him as his kiss deepened, lengthened and possessed. His hands slid the length of her body from her shoulders to her hips, moulding her against him in a slow, sweet fusion that made her tinglingly aware of his desire for her.

'See the effect you have on me,' he whispered. She blushed, hiding her face against him, but he slipped a hand under her chin, forcing it up so that they could kiss again, before he lifted her in his arms and carried her to the settee. Lying half beside him, half across him, she gave herself up to Jason's kisses. His mouth explored the contours of her face, then teased the pulse in her throat. His fingers caressed her bare neck, lingering over the faint mark the chain had made when she snapped it.

'So you didn't need it after all,' he murmured.

'I've worn it for so long, I feel strange without it,' she confessed, aware that her voice was trembling.

'Wear this instead.' He bent his head and pressed his mouth to the shadowed hollow between her breasts where Jeremy's ring had lain.

A long, sweet shiver ran through her entire body, but in spite of herself she felt a growing tension building up deep inside her. Beyond this was the point of no return, and she was frightened of her own inexperience and the demands that might be made of it.

Jason's lips and hands were suddenly asking questions for which she no longer had the answers and finally, with a little cry of protest, she twisted away from the urgency of his caresses and stumbled to her feet, wrapping the housecoat round her body in an instinctive gesture of protectiveness.

'Catriona?' He got up, raking reluctant fingers through his dishevelled hair. 'Darling, what is it?'

'I—I don't know.' Her voice wavered, sounding strained

120

and unfamiliar. 'I—I just—can't . . .' She broke down, covering her face with her hands.

There was a long, grim silence. When at last she ventured to look up, he had moved away to the opposite side of the fireplace, and was standing, smoking a cigarette in quick, jerky puffs.

She felt sick with shame, and her body ached with frustrated emotion. A sudden longing for reassurance swept over her and she moved towards him. 'Jason?'

'Oh God—no!' he exploded. He stepped backwards, throwing up a hand as if he was warding her off, and Catriona paused, shocked and dismayed. 'Not again, thank you. I don't know what effect this stop-go policy of yours is having on you, my sweet, but it's playing hell with my nervous system, so kindly keep your distance.'

'Jason—please. You don't understand . . .'

'I understand all right,' he said. 'You can't be properly grateful until you know the full extent of your obligation, and you feel that gratitude has gone far enough for one night. Well, consider all debts paid and in full. I never did like the instalment system, and where sex is concerned, it's just sheer bloody disaster.'

'*No!*' He was at the door, shrugging on his discarded jacket, but she reached him and gripped his arm, preventing him from turning the latch. 'You must listen to me!'

His mouth curled impatiently. 'You have my undivided attention.'

She looked up at him, her eyes enormous with tears. 'You think I've just been—teasing you, stringing you along so that you'll help me. But it isn't true. Oh, I know you talked about my being under an obligation to you, but you can't imagine I let you—kiss me because I felt—obligated.'

'Then why?' His voice was cynical. 'I'd like to know what you did feel—if anything.'

121

It would have been the easiest thing in the world then to have cried, 'It was because I love you'—the easiest, and yet the most impossible. The only sure thing in a reeling world was that he must never know about this foolish, hopeless love he had engendered in her. She did not know which reaction she would find harder to bear, his mockery or his pity.

'Well, why?' he prompted, his voice harsh.

'I don't know.' She stared unhappily down at the carpet. 'No one had ever touched me like that—or kissed me—before, and I—wanted . . . I thought . . .'

'My God,' he said slowly. He put his hand under her chin forcing her to look up at him again. 'Didn't it occur to you that you were playing with fire? That there's only one inevitable conclusion when a man makes love to a girl as I was to you?'

'I didn't think at first,' she whispered. 'And then, when I did think—I was frightened . . .'

'I see.' He was silent for a moment. 'Did you find me so repulsive, then, or did you merely think I was such a selfish brute that I wouldn't guess how—innocent you were and be gentle with you?'

'Oh, no.' She twisted her hands in the folds of her gown.

'Then I can only conclude that it wasn't just virginal misgivings that made you back off like that, and that you haven't told me the whole reason. Is there something else—something that you're keeping from me?'

'Yes,' she said miserably, knowing that he only had to look into her eyes to see the shaming truth.

'I thought so,' he said quietly. 'It explains a lot, doesn't it? That scene in the kitchen with Jeremy—even your motive for asking me for help as you did.' He gave a short, mirthless laugh. 'You know, you really had me going there for a while. I thought you wanted me, when all you were after was a lesson in loving. Well, next time choose someone else for your naïve little experiments or you may find you're out of your depth.' She cried out in hurt at that, but his voice went on relentlessly. 'Stick to the surface emotions, darling, like that pretty song you sang so sweetly tonight. But leave love out of it. That's too wild a melody for the limits you've imposed on yourself—musically and emotionally.'

If he had struck her, the pain could not have been greater, she thought dully as the door closed behind him.

She walked back to the sofa and sank down on it. The rumpled cushions still bore the impress of his body, and with a little moan she buried her face in them and wept until she could weep no more.

CHAPTER SIX

CATRIONA was dry-eyed but still wide awake an hour later when Sally tiptoed into the bedroom.

'I'm glad you're not asleep.' Sally switched on the lamp on the cabinet that stood between the two beds. 'Whatever happened at Moira's? Everyone's dying of curiosity. The story is that she threw a drink all over you.'

Catriona sighed. 'She did spill one down me,' she admitted. 'I don't know whether it was deliberate or not.'

'Well, if it wasn't this time, it will be next—and she'll probably use vitriol.' Sally's voice was muffled as she tugged her dress over her head. 'She gets you round there as the hired help and you turn into the evening's sensation. Then, to cap it all, you walk off with the man in her life. I've never seen her in such a temper! I don't envy Jason making his peace with her tonight, but,' she chuckled, 'no doubt he has his methods.'

Catriona lay very still, trying to assimilate what had just been said.

'He—went back to the party, then?' she managed, her throat dry.

'Naturally.' Sally got into bed and clicked off the light. 'After all, his invitation would include breakfast as well.'

'I suppose so.' Catriona had no idea how her voice could sound so normal in spite of the pain that seemed to be tearing her apart.

'Well, at least no one can ever wonder what they see in each other,' said Sally, punching her pillow into shape. 'And I'm sure it isn't marriage. Even Moira has enough sense to realise that she's wasting her time trying to pin Jason down—so she settles for what she can get.' She yawned. 'Goodnight, love. Happy dreams.'

'Goodnight,' Catriona returned almost inaudibly.

She was still pale and heavy-eyed when she returned to work at the centre the following week. Both Jean and Andrew exclaimed over her wan appearance and she obediently accepted the aspirin and cup of coffee they pressed on her, but firmly declined the suggestion that she should go home again. Work was what she wanted, she thought. Something to occupy her mind and create the physical tiredness that would enable her to sleep at night.

News at the centre was depressing. Andrew had received a letter from the local authority notifying him that the house was to be looked over by a building inspector within the next few days.

'This could be the crunch,' he said worriedly. 'They may condemn the place unless we can carry certain vital work out.'

Catriona remained silent. She was glad that she had not raised Andrew's hopes in any way by telling him she intended to ask Jason's help. It would have been awful to have had to confess what a failure it had been, and impossible to explain why.

Andrew was speaking again. 'There'll be a meeting of the trustees later this week. I'll have to attend and let them know the exact position.' He sighed. 'It isn't a task I relish.'

'What will you do if the centre has to close?' Catriona asked.

He shrugged. 'Go back to parish work, I suppose.'

'And Jean?' She watched him carefully, and had the satisfaction of seeing him flush.

'Well, she's very highly qualified, you know,' he said awkwardly. 'She would have no trouble in getting another post even if—I mean, if she didn't . . .' His voice tailed off and Catriona bent over her typewriter, hiding a smile.

The morning was as busy as she had hoped. The phone rang constantly, usually proving to be social workers urgently seeking accommodation for people, and several new arrivals, including two families with young children, actually took up residence. In the middle of it all, the police arrived to pick up a young man who had arrived over the weekend, after absconding from Borstal, and the builder looked in to announce, with a certain gloomy relish, that the usual patching-up job on the roof was no longer adequate and that an entirely new roof was what was needed.

Jean and Catriona were having a belated snack in the kitchen when two men appeared in the doorway to ask where the piano was wanted.

'Oh, lord!' Jean jumped up. 'I'd forgotten all about it. It had better go in the big sitting room, I suppose.'

As she hurried out to the hall, she explained to Catriona that the piano was a gift from a local youth club which had been fortunate enough to acquire a better one. It was indeed a very battered-looking instrument, with the ivory missing from a number of the keys, but as Catriona tried a few experimental chords, it seemed to be in tune.

'Mrs Lamb will be delighted,' Jean remarked. 'Apparently she used to play in a pub at one time, so I daresay we can look forward to some live entertainment in the evenings.'

125

'I could always bring my guitar along,' Catriona offered rather diffidently.

'That would be marvellous.' Jean looked at her quickly. 'But don't feel you have to. You work quite hard enough in office hours without coming back in your own time.'

'I'd like to.' Catriona picked out a soft minor chord before closing the piano lid. 'I don't have a lot to do in my spare time.' She saw Jean watching her with a concerned expression and gave a determined smile. 'I must get back to work.'

But as they came out into the hall, they saw they had yet another visitor. Mrs Henderson was standing in the hall, her neat, upright figure cast in lines of disapproval.

'Good afternoon, Miss Haydon,' she greeted Jean, and gave Catriona a glacial look. 'And how long do you normally take for a lunch break, young woman?'

'I have an hour,' Catriona told her quietly.

'She usually takes less, but today she was giving me a hand on the domestic side,' Jean intervened, and Catriona looked at her gratefully.

'I see.' Mrs Henderson sniffed slightly. 'The Trust does not pay office worker's wages to domestic staff, Miss Haydon. I had my doubts as to whether a full-time office assistant was really necessary, although Mr Milner assured me she was. If Miss—er—Muir doesn't have sufficient work . . .'

'Oh, but I do,' Catriona protested. 'It was just that the piano arrived and we were trying it.'

She realised at once she had said the wrong thing. Mrs Henderson's mouth grew tighter than ever.

'A piano—what piano?' She listened to Jean's explanation in silence with no relaxation of her attitude. 'I suppose the gift was intended as an act of kindness,' she said at last. 'But I feel the Trustees should have been consulted before it was accepted. After all, Miss Haydon, this is intended to be a shelter for distressed persons, not a social club. However, as it is here now, I suppose it had better stay. Perhaps it had better be locked during working hours.'

Catriona flushed angrily at the implication, but Jean's voice was tranquil as she replied, 'Of course, Mrs Henderson. I'll see to it.'

Mrs Henderson turned her gaze back to Catriona. 'Do you intend to resume work at all this afternoon, young woman?' she asked glacially, and Catriona, her face flaming, walked ahead of her into the office. Andrew, who was sitting at one of the tables, sent her a sympathetic look, but it also contained a warning, and she bit back the protest that was trembling on her lips. Mrs Henderson did not seem to like her very much as it was, and no useful purpose would be served by antagonising her further. She sat down at her typewriter and fitted paper and carbons into it with exaggerated efficiency.

Andrew had risen and welcomed Mrs Henderson, offering her a chair.

'Well, Mr Milner, and have you had time to think over the proposition that has been put to us?'

'Frankly, I've thought about nothing else since you telephoned.' Andrew resumed his own seat. 'It's come rather as a bolt from the blue.'

'It has, indeed,' Mrs Henderson said with a trace of grimness. 'And you are sure you are not responsible?'

'Quite sure.' Andrew shook his head. 'Oh, I've heard of the programme, of course, but I can't imagine why they should want to feature the centre on it.'

'On the contrary, I consider that some tribute to my dear husband's unfailing generosity is long overdue. He certainly never received the recognition he deserved in his lifetime.'

'No.' Andrew was silent for a moment. 'But—forgive me —is this the purpose of the programme? My understanding was that it was the centre itself—alive and working—that they wanted to film.'

Catriona sat as if she had been turned to stone. She

127

turned and her eyes met Andrew's with a mute question. He nodded.

'It's true, Catriona. Incredible as it may sound, Mrs Henderson has been contacted by a television producer who wants to feature the centre in a forthcoming documentary.'

'That—that's wonderful.' Catriona's response was totally mechanical. She did not ask which television station or even which programme was involved. She did not have to ask. She knew.

'Please don't imagine you will be appearing on television, Miss Muir,' Mrs Henderson said acidly. 'The image is the important thing, as the young man who spoke to me was saying, and I want ours to be of the serious Christian work that goes on here to help the—er—under-privileged. I certainly don't wish to give the impression that it is merely a rest-home for mini-skirted trendies.'

Catriona glanced down in surprise at her own knee-length skirt, but she decided it would be unwise to venture any retort. Besides, she had other things to concern her, apart from Mrs Henderson's overt disapproval. She began to type again, feeling she was in a dream. It was surely too much of a coincidence for the approach from the television company not to have come from Jason Lord, yet at the same time she could hardly believe it. She had told herself so many times since that disastrous evening that she could not expect ever to see or hear from him again, and she had totally discounted the idea that he might still be prepared to help the centre. She felt she only had herself to blame for this—that she should have known that a personal appeal from herself was bound to be misunderstood, that in Jason's cynical world, no one gave anything for nothing. So what explanation was there for this apparent change of heart? She could think of none.

'What puzzles me,' Andrew was saying, 'is how they got on to us in the first place.' Catriona tensed slightly.

'I am more gratified than puzzled.' Mrs Henderson rose,

shaking the creases out of her skirt. 'It proves that our efforts here are not going entirely unnoticed, and that someone has realised we have a valuable contribution to make in helping to plug some of the gaps left by the social services and the government.'

Andrew looked a little taken aback at hearing what were virtually his own words quoted back at him. Then he cleared his throat.

'While we're on the subject of plugging gaps,' he said awkwardly, 'the builder was here this morning and he left this estimate for doing the roof. It—it's rather costly, I'm afraid. I intended to send it on to the Trustees tonight, but as you're here . . .'

Mrs Henderson took it and gave it a perfunctory glance. 'I'll see it is put on the agenda for this week's meeting,' she said. 'But as I've warned you, Mr Milner, I can hold out no hope for outlay of this kind being sanctioned.'

'I thought in view of the fact that we'll be having TV cameras descending on us shortly——' Andrew began, but Mrs Henderson cut in.

'They will hardly be concerned with photographing the roof,' she said coldly. 'Besides, I have no wish for the centre to present a misleading appearance of affluence.'

'I don't think anyone will mistake it for a luxury hotel.' Andrew's voice was equally cool.

'I hope not indeed.' Mrs Henderson put on her gloves. 'I understand the producer or his assistant will be calling on you in the next few days to arrange the filming. I'm sure you will give them your co-operation.'

'Naturally, I shall do my best.' Andrew escorted her to the door and they went out together, leaving Catriona alone with her turbulent thoughts.

Her first impulse was to hand in her resignation, and so avoid the pain and humiliation of having to face Jason again, but she realised this would be unfair on Andrew. If she went, there was no guarantee that she would be replaced, in fact Mrs Henderson's attitude suggested the opposite, and Andrew had enough to do without having to type and keep the office accounts. She sighed. The only alternative seemed to be to make herself as unobtrusive as possible while the programme was being made. They would both be busy, after all, and it should not be too difficult to keep out of his way. Besides, he would have no more wish to see her than she had to see him, she told herself defiantly and tried to ignore the hurt that rose involuntarily at the thought.

She forced her concentration back to the work she was doing and was typing busily when the office door reopened and Andrew came in with Jean.

'Look at her!' Andrew teased. 'Not even the prospect of being on television can shake our Catriona. She takes it all in her stride.'

Catriona sighed inwardly, but she was relieved that she gave at least an outward appearance of tranquillity. She was even more thankful that she had given no hint to Andrew that she could be involved in the decision to televise the centre. He and Jean would naturally be curious and she could imagine the sort of cross-examination that, with the best intentions, she would be subjected to. Eventually there would be questions that it would hurt too much to answer— explanations that it would embarrass her too much to give. A little voice inside her reminded her that these would become inevitable when Jason arrived at the centre and it became clear that they knew each other, but by then she might have found some kind of defensive armour for herself. At the moment she felt totally vulnerable.

She dragged her attention back to the other two, and the conservation which had now switched, more prosaically, to the gift of the piano.

'I think we ought to christen it with some sort of party,' Andrew suggested. 'What about it, Catriona? Can you organise a *ceilidh* for us?'

'No problem,' Catriona said promptly. 'But will everyone want to join in?'

'Mrs Lamb certainly will, for one,' said Jean. 'She found a stack of ancient sheet music in the stool, and she's been practising ever since. Haven't you heard her?'

Catriona hesitated. 'I was thinking of Mitch, actually. Do we ask her to take part?'

'No harm in asking, I suppose,' said Andrew. 'But I doubt if you'll get an answer.'

Jean sighed. 'Yet she must be interested in music, or else why the guitar?'

'I'd like to think you were right.' Andrew gave a slight frown. 'So far no one's managed to persuade her to touch as much as a string since she's been here. I sometimes wonder if it is hers, or if she even knows how to play it.'

Catriona had been wondering much the same thing. She had observed Mitch a few times since their encounter the previous week and although the girl cradled the guitar as though it was precious to her, she did not hold it as a musician would. It was a mystery, she thought, remembering Mitch's pale, ravaged face and her air of hostile withdrawal.

Sally greeted the idea of the *ceilidh* with enthusiasm when Catriona mentioned it as they ate their meal that evening.

'Let me know when it is, and I'll come and bring some of the others as well,' she suggested. 'Ian and Barbara both sing, and the rest of us could maybe do some improvisations. Could be very therapeutic,' she added largely, waving a salad-laden fork.

Catriona was amused. 'For whom?'

Sally laughed back at her. 'Everyone.' She eyed Catriona. 'You look as if you could use some therapy yourself, love. What's up?'

Catriona looked down at her plate. 'Nothing.'

Sally shrugged. 'Have it your own way. I won't pry.' She gave Catriona a narrow look. 'On second thoughts, perhaps

131

I will. You're not pining for Jeremy Lord, are you?'

'Jeremy?' Catriona gasped, then flushed hotly. 'Oh, no—really. Nothing like that.'

'Then it's worse than I thought.' Sally speared a sliver of cucumber with an abstracted jab. 'Falling for Jeremy is like getting 'flu in February—one of life's minor hazards and nasty while it lasts—which luckily it doesn't. But if it isn't Jeremy then it must be someone else.' She groaned. 'And I was hoping you'd fall for Ian.'

Catriona smiled faintly. 'He's—very nice.'

'Ugh! That sounds more like a verdict than an opinion,' Sally made a comical grimace. 'Poor Ian, he deserves better than that. But something tells me this is not a good time for girlish confidences. Are you feeling very raw?'

Catriona nodded, not trusting herself to speak.

'Then we'll change the subject. How do you feel about having a third girl here?'

'A third? Catriona was diverted in spite of herself. 'Where would we put her?'

'Amazing as it may seem, there is just room in the bedroom, although the chest of drawers would have to come in here. Julie at the club is looking for a new place and she'd like to join up with us. It would help with the rent and also be company for you when I go on tour, which could be quite soon. But I told her there was nothing doing until I'd consulted you.'

'The more the merrier,' Catriona agreed. 'I've no objection.'

'Good—then I'll let her know.' Sally pushed her plate away and leaned back in her chair. 'Robbie came to the club at lunchtime today. He was looking for you.'

'Robbie?'

Catriona wrinkled her brow.

'Your accompanist at Moira's party. He's been singing your praises to some of his contacts in the profession, and it seems he could get you an audition. It might mean a job in a club he has an interest in—apparently they use a lot of new talent.'

'I don't think I want that,' Catriona said slowly.

'Don't be mad, love. It could be your big break. He thinks you have a real voice in the making.'

Catriona shook her head. 'I don't fool myself, Sally. I was a big hit at home, but here in London girl folk singers are ten a penny. I'll stick to the job I'm doing, and sing for pleasure.'

Or for pain. '*I know who I love, But the dear knows who I'll marry.*'

'Well, any way.' Sally hunted in her bag and produced a small business card. 'Here's his phone number, just in case you change your mind.'

'I don't think I shall.' Catriona accepted the card and tucked it into her purse.

'You certainly stick to your guns!' Sally gave a little sigh. 'If I had your principles, I think I'd be forever tripping over them.'

'Mine aren't always very comfortable,' Catriona said for-lornly. 'But sometimes they're all I have.'

The next couple of days dragged by and Catriona felt on edge each hour she spent at the centre. It was inevitable that the forthcoming visit from the television crew should be on everyone's minds and form the main topic of conversation, but she found it no help at all to her peace of mind. She found she was beginning to look towards the window every time a vehicle drew up in the street outside, and chided her-self for being ridiculous.

When the blue and white vans with their 'Home Counties TV' signs drew up outside the centre, it was almost an anti-climax. The tall figure her eyes instinctively sought was not among the gang of cameramen, sound recordists and other personnel who came tramping into the building, laden with equipment. The man who appeared to be in charge introduced himself as Garfield Lucas, and although Catriona eavesdropped shamelessly on his ensuing conversation with Andrew, she did not hear Jason Lord's name mentioned once, although she ascertained that the film on the centre was intended for the *Here and Now* programme which he produced and presented.

'The film will be followed by a live studio discussion in front of an invited audience,' Lucas told them. 'We hope that representatives of other charitable organisations will be there, as well as your own residents and staff. And Mrs Henderson will be interviewed, of course.'

He put a hand on Andrew's shoulder and steered him out of the room, talking volubly as he went. A few minutes later, Jean's head popped round the door.

'They're "familiarising themselves" with the place,' she said rather faintly, dropping into a chair. 'I just hope the wiring can stand it. I have a feeling that when they plug in that equipment, we may all blow sky-high.'

Catriona sighed under her breath. Sooner or later she would have to confess the part she had played in all this disruption, she thought. It was all a far cry from the short, dignified Sunday evening appeal she had originally visualised.

Andrew reappeared, looking harassed. 'Is there a chance of any coffee, Jean? They probably all drink gallons of the stuff.'

'I'll come and see to it now.' Jean jumped up, and they went out together.

Catriona applied herself to typing the centre's accounts for the Trustees' meeting, the following day. She was so engrossed that she failed to hear anyone enter the room and only the uneasy feeling that she was being watched eventually caused her to lift her eyes from her work.

The girl Mitch was standing behind the door, her guitar in her arms. She was very pale, and her eyes, as they met Catriona's, looked hunted. Catriona bit her lip. She had not gauged the effect the intrusion of cameras and crew might have on someone like Mitch when she had embarked on this crusade for publicity.

Trying to sound casual, she said, 'Have you popped in here for some peace? I don't blame you. There's a chair over there, between the filing cabinets.'

She removed her work from the machine, and began to check it through, studiously avoiding looking at Mitch, but a flicker of movement told her that Mitch had taken the chair she had pointed out. For a while there was silence, but eventually Catriona had to go to the stationery cupboard to get a fresh box of envelopes. Mitch was sitting, staring at the floor, her hands loosely clasped round her knees. The guitar was standing on the floor beside her, resting against one of the cabinets.

Catriona paused. 'That's a genuine Spanish guitar, isn't it?' she asked, trying to sound friendly without being pushing. She waited and was rewarded with the slightest affirmative movement of Mitch's head.

'I have a guitar too, but it's nothing like as good as that one,' she said, after a pause. 'Could I—could I have a look at yours?'

It was almost like standing on the edge of a precipice, waiting for the puff of wind that could send you to destruction. She remembered that Mitch had been driven to violence once already over this very guitar. She was only the office typist, for heaven's sake. Why was she trying to play psychologist to this girl who could well be seriously disturbed? She waited uneasily, expecting Mitch to snatch the guitar up and nurse it against her in the usual way. For a moment Mitch's hand went out, half protectively, then she withdrew it again.

Catriona took a deep breath. 'May I look at it?'

A long, long pause. Then that barely discernible nod again. Catriona felt as if she was tiptoeing on eggshells as she walked across to the guitar and picked it up. Mitch went on staring at the floor, as if she was totally oblivious to what was going on. Catriona tried a tentative chord and winced.

'It's very out of tune,' she said. 'You ought to tune it, Mitch. It's a shame to leave it in this state—a lovely thing like this. Do you know how to tune it?'

She looked down at Mitch and found the other girl's eyes fixed on her with a strange intensity, but she did not move or make any sign. Catriona tried again. 'Shall I tune it for you?'

She made a few swift adjustments. 'Now listen.' Once again her fingers touched the strings, and this time they sang for her. She stilled them and put the guitar back on the floor beside Mitch.

'We're going to have a bit of a *ceilidh* here one night,' she said. 'Why don't you come and bring your guitar? We'd love to hear you play it.'

'No.' It was a ragged breath of sound. Mitch picked up the guitar and lifted herself from the chair in one panic-stricken movement. She flew to the door, only to find her way blocked.

'I beg your pardon,' Jason's voice was courteous, as he stood aside to let her pass. He watched her flying figure disappear up the stairs and turned back to Catriona, his brows lifted inquiringly.

'I'm looking for Mr Milner,' he said.

Catriona swallowed. 'I—I'll go and find him for you.'

'Thank you.' He took off his leather coat and hung it on the back of a chair, before wandering across to the window and standing looking out, with his back turned to her. They could have been strangers, she thought incredulously. For a dreadful moment, she thought she might burst into tears, then she managed to control herself and jutted her chin. If that was the way he wanted it, then that was fine with her.

She found Andrew, looking hunted, in the kitchen and told him the programme producer was waiting in the office, before helping Jean serve the remaining coffees and explain what was happening to the residents who were around.

Mrs Lamb was inclined to be belligerent. 'Well, no one asked us if we wanted it,' she said. 'I'm not going to be treated like an animal in a zoo, thank you very much.'

Calming ruffled sensibilities and soothing apprehensions took some time, and when Catriona eventually went reluctantly back to the office, Jason had gone. But her feeling of relief was shortlived. Andrew informed her that there was to be a script conference that afternoon, and that Jason had asked if the centre would provide secretarial back-up, as his own girl was off sick.

'I told him I was sure it would be all right,' Andrew said, a belatedly dubious note creeping into his voice. 'Do you think you can cope, Catriona? He seems a pretty high-powered operator.'

Catriona sighed. 'I haven't much choice, have I?' she said tautly.

She felt icy with nerves as they all gathered round one of the tables in the office that afternoon, but the anticipation proved worse than the event. Jason briefly outlined the format of the filming he proposed, and asked Andrew if there were any additions or criticism he wanted to make. The emphasis was to be on the residents, and the role the centre was playing in their lives at a time of personal crisis. It was a far cry from the tribute to the late Mr Henderson that his widow had envisaged, Catriona thought, masking her amusement.

'Coupled with this will, of course, be the crisis in the centre's own affairs.' Jason stared down at the pencil he was holding.

'I wouldn't put it quite as strongly as that,' Andrew said rather stiffly.

'Oh?' Jason raised his brows. 'And how precisely would you put it? You see, Mr Milner, we've been doing some homework. We've spoken to some of the trustees, apart from Alice Henderson, and also to some of the local council officials. Their views coincide. They feel the centre's days could be numbered, unless the situation alters radically and soon.'

Catriona stared down at her notebook and the neat short-hand symbols swam meaninglessly in front of her eyes. She felt like Judas. What had she told him so recklessly that night? That the end justified the means. She was no longer sure of that.

'There is a problem with cash,' Andrew admitted quietly.

'I think it's more than a problem, Mr Milner,' Jason said almost gently. 'From what I've been told, the Trust is almost broke. I've also been told that a rescue operation to attract more money could have started a long time ago, but for the—intransigent attitude of Mrs Henderson herself. Am I correct?' He paused, but Andrew made no reply. 'It seems that I am.'

Andrew gave him a steady look. 'I suppose this explains the sudden interest of the media in our affairs—like vultures in at the death.'

Jason eyed him ironically. 'What do you expect, Mr Milner? This place and the work you do here isn't exactly unique, you know. We could have put the spotlight on a dozen such places—but we chose you. Did you never ask yourself why? You know the situation better than anyone. Perhaps it's time you faced up to it realistically.'

He looked down at the notepad in front of him. 'Of course, it's still not too late. If you want us to go . . .'

Catriona sent Andrew a stricken look. He might not like the angle that the programme was going to take, but it might be their last and only opportunity to arouse public interest in their plight. If Andrew turned it down, she could see no hope for the centre or the people who depended on it.

Andrew shook his head slowly. 'I don't think the choice is mine,' he said. 'We need any help we can get, whether there are strings attached or not, and we'll grant you—every facility.'

'Thanks.' Jason's tone was noncommittal. 'Well, we'd better make a start.'

Catriona felt physically and mentally exhausted as she pulled the last sheets out of the typewriter two hours later. The conference had made demands on her capabilities, and no concessions had been made for her lack of experience. But she had struggled on doggedly, pride refusing to allow her to admit that she was having difficulties under Jason's mocking gaze. She had a strong feeling that the speed at which the discussion had been taken, interspersed with the instructions that had been almost carelessly flung at her, had been intended to show how inadequate she was, but this had made her all the more determined not to ask him to slow down, or repeat anything.

'Finished?' His hand came over her shoulder, reaching for the papers, and she started violently. She had not heard him enter the office. She was disturbed by his sudden proximity as he stood behind her chair, reading through the notes, and she made herself draw away, moving her chair slightly, so that there was no tantalising physical contact between them. She glanced up at him involuntarily as she did so, and saw by the slight twist of his mouth that the movement had not gone unnoticed.

'Very neat,' he said briefly, tossing the sheets back on the desk. 'I'll take the top copy with me tonight, and you can give a carbon to Lucas, if you will.'

'Of course,' she said colourlessly, wishing that she could adopt the same impersonality towards him.

'Right,' he glanced at his watch. 'I have a few letters, when you're ready.'

He began dictating almost before Catriona had time to open her pad and reach for her pencil. It was more like an endurance test than dictation, she thought furiously.

'I'd like those to go tonight,' he said casually when he had finished. 'They shouldn't take you long.'

Catriona stole a surreptitious glance at her own watch and

saw resignedly that it was past the time she should have left for home. She stifled a sigh as she assembled papers and carbons.

'I'm not keeping you, am I?' His voice was bland. 'But your—er—boss did promise me every facility and . . .'

'It's all right,' she interrupted flatly, winding the paper into the machine. She forced herself to concentrate on the task in hand, willing herself to ignore the fact that Jason had drawn up a chair, and had put his feet up on the edge of her table. But the knowledge of his scrutiny made her flying fingers stumble, and she flushed with annoyance and embarrassment as she was forced to take a fresh sheet.

'Would you mind not watching me?' she appealed at last.

'I'm sorry.' He raised his eyebrows. 'Diane isn't quite so sensitive. She's used to me breathing down her neck.'

Catriona remained silent. Was that meant to imply, she wondered bitterly, that Diane had been on equally intimate terms with him and yet was able to transfer their relationship to a purely business footing in the office? If so, it required a degree of sophistication that she simply did not possess. She was tormented by her constant awareness of his masculinity.

'I'll seek out Jean and see if I can raise some coffee.' He got to his feet, stretching. 'Would you like some?'

Perversely ignoring the cravings of her empty stomach, she shook her head.

'I see. I'm to get out and keep out.' His voice mocked, then paused as if awaiting her retaliation, but she made no reply and after a moment she heard the office door close behind him.

By the time his letters were completed and ready for his signature, he still had not returned and Catriona was forced to go in search of him. She eventually ran him to earth in the kitchen, sitting at the big central table and chatting to Jean and some of the women residents, Mrs Lamb among them. Judging by the rapt look on Mrs Lamb's face and the way

140

she seemed to be hanging on his every word, Catriona surmised that all her earlier feelings about being an animal in a zoo had been forgotten, and she was not altogether surprised when Mrs Lamb excitedly revealed that she and her family were to be the subject of one of the in-depth interviews that Jason had planned for the programme. Catriona saw Jean smile and wink and smiled, a little resignedly, in response. It was inevitable that Jason would win, she thought. She should be glad that his victory had not included herself.

He accompanied her back to the office and she waited quietly while he checked the letters and added his bold, uncompromising signature to them.

'I've made you late,' he said abruptly. 'Can I give you a lift?'

'No, thank you.' She was glad she was folding the letters and putting them into their envelopes. It gave her an excuse to keep her face averted.

'You'll be quite safe,' Jason jeered. 'I rarely rape women while I'm driving. London traffic doesn't permit it, for one thing.'

She flushed unhappily and ventured a glance at him. 'Please don't be funny.'

'Is that what I am?' he said. 'I'll take your word for it, though I'm sure as hell not laughing.'

He reached out suddenly and took her arm, bruising her flesh under the hard pressure of his fingers. 'Catriona.'

She was frightened—frightened of the suppressed violence she could hear in his voice, and the equal violence of her own reaction to this relatively minor physical contact with him. She ached with the need to turn to him, to press herself against him—and with the absolute necessity to do the opposite—to stay aloof and give no hint of the furore that even his slightest touch could create in her.

Andrew's voice from the doorway was like a sudden deluge of cold water. 'Is anything the matter?'

'Nothing.' Catriona pulled herself free as soon as she felt Jason's grip slacken. 'Mr—Mr Lord was just going.'

She hated the almost pleading note that she knew had entered her voice and she stared down at the floor, unwilling to meet Jason's glance but aware that he was standing watching her, hands on hips. After what seemed like an eternity, he picked his leather coat off the back of a chair, slung it across his shoulder and, with a terse goodnight to Andrew, walked out.

There was a long silence, then Andrew said quietly, 'Do you want to talk about it?'

'There's nothing to talk about,' she said drearily.

'But you and Lord aren't exactly—strangers?'

'No,' she admitted, her gaze still fixed on the floor.

'I see.' Andrew paused. 'It explains a lot, however.'

'I suppose I would have told you eventually,' she said unhappily. 'But I have felt dreadful about unleashing—all this on to you. I just didn't expect it to happen like this.'

'I know. It just seemed like a good idea at the time.' She looked up quickly and saw that he was smiling at her. 'My dear girl, don't look so stricken. I know you've acted with the very best of intentions, and I'm sure that when we've all had time to catch our breath, we'll realise even more that the centre can only benefit in the end. It just takes some getting used to, when you're not used to their methods. One thing I'll say for your Mr Lord—he seems to have some winning ways about him.'

Catriona winced inwardly. 'He's not my Mr Lord,' she said with some constraint.

'No?' Andrew sighed. 'It's all right, Catriona. I won't pry into your business. I have absolutely no right to cross-examine you any way. Get along home now. It's going to be another full day tomorrow. I just hope we all bear up under the strain.'

'So do I,' she said almost inaudibly. 'So do I.'

142

CHAPTER SEVEN

IT was surprising how quickly they all became used to the film crew being in their midst. Before two days had passed, the cameras, microphones and cables seemed like part of the ordinary furnishings, and Lucas and the others were like old friends.

Diane, Jason's secretary, had recovered from her virus and was back at work, taking much of the pressure from Catriona, who did not know whether to be glad or sorry. No matter how much she might tell herself that her feelings for Jason were a total waste of time, she still could not deny their existence, and it was difficult to maintain the aloof pose she had adopted for her own protection when he was around. Not that she had had much opportunity to do anything else. Jason had offered her no more lifts or given any suggestion that their relationship had ever been on anything but a business level.

She saw less of him too now that filming had started. Diane worked where he was, balancing a portable typewriter on any surface that offered, and rarely used the office at all. Catriona tried to force her concentration back on to the run-of-the-mill office routine, mentally kicking herself every time a strange step sounded in the hall outside and she looked hopefully towards the door. She was rarely completely alone, however. Mitch now spent most of her day crouching, head bent, on the painted kitchen chair in between the two filing cabinets, the guitar never far from her feet. Catriona had been shaken the first time she had turned to see the silent girl sitting behind her, her eyes fixed on the floor, but gradually she became used to the almost noiseless opening of the office door and the quiet shuffle of feet that heralded Mitch's arrival.

Eventually, almost in desperation, Catriona began to talk to her. She did not expect any response and she received none. She did not even know if Mitch, sunk in some private world where any contact seemed an intrusion, was aware of the reflective monologue which began at first hesitantly, then with growing confidence, to bombard her. Sometimes Catriona, listening almost in astonishment to the jumble of thoughts and commentary on her activities issuing from her own mouth, decided that she must be mad, talking to herself like this for the benefit of a girl who seemed totally oblivious to her efforts. She was on the point of deciding that the whole idea was a complete waste of time when Mitch suddenly lifted her head and looked at her. Catriona's voice faltered while her heart gave a sudden, painful leap. Just for that second there had been a look in Mitch's eyes which had suggested that for the first time she had registered Catriona as a separate being. It would have been an exaggeration to describe it as a flash of interest, but there had been—something, the faintest of communications perhaps, but more hopeful than any of the vague head movements that had been Catriona's earlier experience.

She mentioned it to Andrew when next she saw him alone, but though he was pleased at her interest and concern, she could see that he was sceptical.

'Don't raise your hopes too high, Catriona,' he warned. 'Jean and I have thought several times we might be on the edge of a breakthrough with her, but each time she retreats back into that shell of hers. I don't want you to be disheartened if it happens to you.'

Catriona kept his words firmly at the forefront of her mind during her next encounter with Mitch, but she still felt hopeful. She kept the flood of inconsequential chatter going, and at times she saw Mitch was watching her with an almost puzzled expression in her eyes, like someone who has inadvertently tuned into a foreign radio station and is trying to recognise the language.

It was getting harder all the time, finding things to say. Catriona had dealt with her work at the centre, her friendship with Sally and even her visit to the television centre and her singing debut at Moira Dane's party, and it was oddly painful to discover how many quite innocuous reminiscences could suddenly produce their own no-go areas. It would be altogether too tempting to use the silent Mitch as a sounding board for the wild confusion of her feelings about Jason. She was somehow certain that she needed to put this confusion into words, to hear herself describe the pain, the loneliness and the sheer wanting that assailed her day and night. But at the same time she knew this was not the time and Mitch was far from being the right person to receive these confidences. One day there would be someone she could tell and then she would be healed, she told herself.

It was inevitable that eventually she should turn back to Aunt Jessie and the days in Torvaig, and this brought its own but different pain. It was as if she was reciting the details of someone else's life, someone else's experience. As if the things that had happened to her since she reached London were the only reality, and the thought brought guilt and bewilderment in its wake. I am the same person, she cried out to herself silently, but she knew it was not true, and that in a matter of weeks she had changed irrevocably from the girl who had set out with such blithe naïvety. Then, she had known safety and security. Now, her only awareness seemed to be her own uncertainty, and she shivered.

But her introspection vanished when she glanced up and caught Mitch staring at her. She could hardly believe what she saw in the other girl's eyes—a questioning mixed with anticipation as if the silence troubled her. She wants me to go on, Catriona thought, burying her own problems with a

145

swift rush of exhilaration. She actually wants me to go on. Deliberately she hid her delight, resuming her usually casual tone, resisting the temptation to look at Mitch too often, seeking a reaction. Her voice warmed, became slightly husky, as she remembered things—the endless June evenings, the impromptu *ceilidhs*, the smell of baking bread and oat-cakes, the warmth of the sea loch where she had learned to swim—even the bustling quay at Mallaig, the usual focus of holiday treats with Aunt Jessie, where she had stood en-tranced watching the ferries leave for the islands and the fishing boats disgorging their hoards in glittering silver showers.

She only halted when she realised that Mitch was no longer listening, if she ever had been, but was staring instead over her shoulder, her eyes wide and nervous and her body rigid. Catriona swung round and saw Jason was standing in the doorway. He was leaning against the door-post, his hands thrust into his pockets, and he looked as if he had been there for ever.

Catriona felt the colour begin to creep into her face as she nerved herself to meet his cynical regard.

'You paint an idyllic picture, Miss Muir. Perhaps you should offer your services to the Scottish tourist board.'

Catriona bit her lip. 'I do have a job already,' she said quietly.

'Indeed you have—and is this part of it?' Jason glanced significantly at Mitch, who had snatched up her guitar and was obviously on the point of flight.

'I happen to think so.' Catriona watched Mitch's precipi-tate departure with disappointment. It was the old pattern repeating itself, she thought despondently.

Jason watched her go too, then turned back to Catriona. 'I would stick to what you're paid for, Miss Muir.' He nodded towards the elderly typewriter. 'You may break your nails, but your heart should remain intact.'

Out of sight, her hands clenched involuntarily, but she

146

answered him steadily enough. 'Are you trying to tell me not to get involved?'

'Well, that is your usual policy, isn't it?' He produced a packet of cheroots and lit one with deliberation. 'To stay aloof, and make sure you don't allow any feelings intrude. Beware, Catriona. The woman in you could be trying to escape, and that girl could just be the catalyst that will make it happen.'

Hurt prompted her to recklessness. 'You sound bitter, Mr Lord. Could it be because you failed to be the—catalyst yourself?'

'You flatter yourself, darling.' Icy grey eyes seemed to strip her contemptuously. 'Perhaps I wasn't interested enough to exert the necessary pressure.'

Some black angel made her go on. 'Of course, with Miss Dane, you wouldn't need to exert any pressure—would you?'

'You don't really expect me to answer that. I advise you to sheathe your claws, Catriona, before someone decides to clip them for you. Your praiseworthy efforts with that girl don't make you an expert on human nature.'

She bent her head, feeling tears prick at the back of her eyelids. 'I'm sorry,' she apologised constrictedly.

'Forget it,' he said briefly. 'May I use the telephone in here?'

'Yes, of course.' Struggling for self-control, she moved hurriedly away from the table. 'Is it private—I mean, do you want me to leave the room while you make your call?'

He shrugged. 'It's up to you. I'm calling Miss Dane, as a matter of fact, to invite her to have dinner with me tonight. Perhaps you'd like to stick around and see how much pressure I have to exert.'

She said in a stifled voice, 'Thank you—no.' She was past him and at the door even before he had begun to dial.

Andrew met her as she crossed the hall, making for the kitchen.

147

'Oh, Catriona.' He was looking harassed. 'Lucas wants to know if we can fix the *ceilidh* for tomorrow night. He wants to wrap up the filming, apparently, and feels the *ceilidh* would be a lighthearted contrast to other elements in the programme.'

'Heavens!' she stared at him, dismayed. 'I—I didn't imagine they would want to film that. Does Mrs Henderson know?'

Andrew's lips tightened slightly. 'I don't think she does. Lucas and Jason Lord have both been in contact with her, it seems, and asked her to come to the centre to be interviewed against its background—chatting with the residents, helping around—that sort of thing. She refused point blank— said she would prefer to be interviewed at her own home, or during the studio discussion after the programme.' He sighed. 'I think she's making a big mistake. She's drawn her own conclusions about the way the programme is being slanted, and I'm afraid she's in for a shock. If she'd only come down and co-operated, at least she would have been forewarned.'

Catriona agreed rather forlornly. She wished that the idea of the *ceilidh* could be forgotten altogether, but she realised that the residents would be disappointed if she backed out now. Their enjoyment and the fostering of a community spirit among them was surely more important than some future accusation of attention-seeking from Mrs Henderson, she decided.

She stayed away from the office for as long as she could without neglecting her work. She did not want to run the risk of overhearing any part of Jason's conversation with Moira Dane. When she finally went back to her desk, the room was empty and the only sign of his presence was the half-smoked cheroot stubbed carelessly out in the ashtray. She wished that emotions could be stifled in the same way.

She worked late that evening, helping Andrew prepare

148

yet another balance sheet for yet another trustees' meeting.

'I asked Mrs Henderson if the meeting could possibly be held over until after the programme had gone out, but she said she didn't see that it could possibly make any difference,' he said gloomily.

'Oh, Andrew!' Impulsively, she laid her hand on his arm. 'It will make a difference. It must. Isn't the whole thing slanted to show how desperately in need of funds the centre is?'

'Yes—Lucas hasn't pulled any punches about that, and the interviews with the residents have produced some really telling stuff.' He smiled slightly. 'To be honest, I never realised how much they thought of the place. We've never asked for thanks, or wanted them particularly. Being taken for granted is just part of the picture—for Jean and myself. But I've been very wrong about that. The majority of the people here take nothing for granted. It was something I needed to be reminded about.'

He put the completed sheets into a cardboard folder.

'Thanks for all this. Some of the telly people are still about. Shall I see if I can wangle you a lift?'

'No.' Catriona shook her head. 'I'm in no great hurry. I rang Sally and warned her I was going to be late, and I think we're going to make do with a Chinese take-away meal tonight.'

She collected her handbag and walked out into the hall, only to come face to face with Moira Dane, strikingly dressed in midnight blue chiffon. She groaned inwardly as she saw hostility replace recognition in Moira's narrowed eyes. If she'd had the least idea that Jason was going to meet her at the centre for their evening together, she would have hidden somewhere, she thought.

'You again!' Moira's tone was frosty. 'What are you doing here?' She looked round at the peeling paintwork. 'Is this where you live?'

149

Catriona held on to her temper with an effort. 'No, Miss Dane. I live with Sally Fenton,' she said quietly. 'But I work here—in the office.'

'I see.' The curves of Moira's mouth became more petulant. 'I wondered why Jason had picked on this place. I suppose this was the sob-story you were feeding him in my kitchen the other night?' She gave her surroundings another disparaging stare. 'My God, what a dump! It should be pulled down rather than saved—but perhaps that's what Jason's going to say on the programme.'

'I don't think so.' Catriona tried to suppress the swift alarm that Moira's words roused in her. 'He's on our side—the whole crew are . . .'

Moira laughed contemptuously. 'The whole crew do what Jason tells them, my child, and Jason does as he pleases. He's not on—your side, or anyone else's if it comes to that. He's a journalist through and through, and he knows a good story when he sees it. If he's taking an interest in this place, it won't be on philanthropic grounds, I can promise you that. It's because he's discovered something which will translate well into television terms—mismanagement of some kind—women and children sleeping in a potential fire trap—that sort of thing. He wouldn't be bothering with it otherwise. And whatever it is that he's found, he'll blow the lid right off.' She looked at Catriona and her smile was pure malice. 'Something tells me, Miss—er—Muir, that you're going to wish that you'd held your tongue.'

Catriona was very white. She said slowly, 'I don't believe you.'

Moira shrugged. 'That's your privilege, my dear. But don't say you weren't warned. And I'd get Sally to show you where the nearest employment exchange is. I think you may need it.'

'What does Miss Muir need?' Jason came strolling from the back of the house, his coat flung casually across one shoulder.

'A better job than this, I would have thought.' Moira turned to him, smiling easily. 'Can we go now? My skin simply crawls in places like this.'

He took her hand and carried it to his lips. 'We can't have that,' he said, and his voice was a caress, Catriona thought miserably. She wanted to confront him with Moira's insinuations, but she decided it was useless. If Moira was lying then he would be pardonably angry, but if she was telling the truth, all he need do was issue a denial. Either way, Catriona could prove nothing. And if she told Andrew, it would simply burden him with yet another worry, she thought wearily.

'Darling.' Moira lifted her hand to Jason's cheek in a smilingly intimate gesture. 'You haven't shaved—really!'

'I'll shave later.' He took her arm and began to guide her towards the door. 'It's going to be a long evening. Good night, Miss Muir. Can we drop you anywhere?'

Catriona shook her head, too unhappy even to reply. She hung back waiting for them to get clear before making her own departure and heard Moira's laugh float back on the evening air.

The anxiety over Jason's motives in making the documentary at the centre stayed with her during a restless night, and still hung there like a black cloud as she arrived for work the following day. But she had little time for brooding. Andrew had gone out and left some work for her, and when that was completed Jean put her head round the door with an appeal for help with the preparations for the *ceilidh*.

Catriona was thankful for the diversion. Mrs Lamb and some of the other women were already hard at work, turning out the big sitting room and sprucing it up for the evening's festivities. There was laughter and chat and occasionally ribald badinage with members of the television crew and Catriona thought that whatever effect the documentary

151

might have on the centre and the lives of the people who lived and worked there, at least it had brought a feeling of hope, no matter how temporary. The centre seemed to have taken on a new lease of life, and there was an air of cheerfulness and optimism which had been sadly lacking when Catriona had first arrived there.

And for all this, Jason Lord was responsible, she thought bitterly. He had made these people trust him, made them believe he was there to help, and now he could just as easily destroy that trust and the spirit of hope that he had fostered. And if he did, she could blame no one but herself. She had involved him, after all, ignoring his warnings that his solution to the centre's problems might not be an acceptable one. She had forgotten that his point of view would be that of the objective journalist—the man who listened to all sides but stayed aloof from personal involvement, and whose judgment might be that the centre was a quixotic adventure, doomed to failure through the inexperience of its administrators.

She went slowly through to the kitchen where Jean had embarked on a massive baking session. Catriona borrowed an overall and assumed responsibility for the sausage rolls. She had always enjoyed cooking and baking at home in Torvaig and had often wished that space in the flat permitted more than mere basic meal preparation.

'This is the first party we've ever had at the centre,' Jean said, removing a tray of small cakes from the oven and transferring them with swift expertise to a wire cooling tray. 'There's never seemed a great deal to celebrate in the past, but now——' she gave Catriona a quick smile—'suddenly everything's on the up and up. Even . . .' She paused suddenly and Catriona was surprised to see her blushing slightly. 'Oh, why shouldn't you be the first to know, Catriona? Andrew and I are going to be married.'

'You and Andrew—oh, but that's wonderful!'

Jean grinned at her, her blush deepening. 'Yes, that's

what we think. We've both known for ages, but Andrew wouldn't ask me before because he felt the future of the centre was too uncertain. But now he feels much happier about the whole thing, and we can start to make some plans of our own.'

Catriona carefully stood the mixing bowl she was washing on the draining board. 'But if the worst did happen—I mean, if the centre did have to close for some reason—it wouldn't make any difference, would it? You would still marry Andrew.'

'Oh yes, eventually. But I suppose the diocese would transfer him to parish work and it would be a matter of waiting until something suitable came along, and I would need to work as well, for a while at least.' Jean was silent for a moment. 'We will move on, of course. The centre won't be our whole lives and I don't think it should be. Places like this need regular infusions of new blood, new ideas. But we would like to see the place safely on its course before we go.'

'Are you going to announce your engagement at the party tonight?'

'Heavens, no!' Jean's face crumpled with amusement. 'They all know anyway. Mrs Lamb's been dropping hints for days. But we're not really having an engagement proper. One of Andrew's friends is part of a team ministry in this parish and he's going to marry us quietly one day.'

That would be like heaven, Catriona thought, to walk off one day hand in hand with the man you loved to a nearby church and return as his wife. Her hands faltered slightly and she dropped a handful of wet utensils back in the sink with a clatter.

One thing was certain, it would be most unfair to burden Jean at this happy moment in her life with the doubts and misgivings which were pressing on her. This would have to be her own personal load of mischief and she would have to bear it.

Mitch was hunched in her usual place in the office when she got back and Catriona plunged into one of her monologues with a feeling of relief. She told Mitch about Jean and Andrew's wedding plans, and described the refreshments she had been helping to make for the *ceilidh* and then launched without preamble into a more detailed account of the *ceilidh* itself and the songs she planned to sing and the part she hoped the others would play.

'And you must come too, Mitch,' she said breathlessly at last. 'And bring your guitar. I'm counting on you.'

She glanced at the other girl as she spoke, but Mitch seemed to have retired back into her private world and hardly seemed to be aware she was there.

From the doorway, Jason said drily, 'Do you really imagine she'll come?'

Catriona swung round to face him, her hand going to her throat. He had occupied her thoughts so exclusively all morning that it was almost shocking to find him actually there, only a few feet away from her.

Her chin went up defiantly. 'And why not?'

His eyes went reflectively from her to her totally passive companion. 'I'd like to think you were right. It's an intriguing situation and has all sorts of possibilities.'

'Within the context of the programme, of course,' she said sarcastically, quoting a phrase she had heard Lucas use at some of the earlier conference sessions.

He raised his eyebrows. 'What else?'

'No,' she said quietly.

'Meaning?'

'I won't let her be—used, as you've used the rest of us,' she said.

He was very still suddenly. 'I wasn't aware of using anyone.'

'Perhaps it's so much second nature to you now that you don't even know when it's happening.'

'Don't run away with the idea that being female gives you

154

some kind of special immunity.' His voice was low and furious. 'You may be able to hand it out, lady, but are you sure you can take it?'

'Quite sure,' she said almost inaudibly. Inside, she was screaming silently—*there's no way you can punish me any more. It's enough that you're here and there's this distance between us. It's punishment enough that I don't have the right to your honesty, that I can't come to you and feel your arms round me.* She closed her eyes against the pain and when she opened them again, Jason had gone and she was alone again with Mitch, still silent, still unmoving, apparently unaware of the tense little scene she had unwittingly provoked.

Catriona began to chatter again, hardly knowing what she was saying. She checked when she caught Mitch's eyes on her, gravely questioning, and realised the salt dampness on her lips was her own tears.

Both Jean, and Andrew when he came back a little while later, insisted that she should go home and take something for the headache she had invented on the spur of the moment.

'I'll take you,' Andrew said firmly, shepherding her towards the door, ignoring her protests that she had work to do.

'But the *ceilidh*——' Catriona resolutely dammed back the tears that were beginning to well up again at their unquestioning kindness, furious at her own weakness.

'We'll get by,' Jean assured her. 'Don't forget your friend Sally and her theatre club crowd are coming to help out. You've done more than enough already. Just have a good rest.'

But that, Catriona found, was easier said than done. Alone at the flat, she roamed about restlessly doing small, aimless bits of tidying up, washing some tights, and preparing herself some scrambled eggs which she did not want. Later, she went out and bought a newspaper and read it conscientiously

155

from cover to cover without absorbing a single word. She tried to do the crossword and abandoned it in irritation because the clues and little squares kept merging into a meaningless jumble in front of her abstracted eyes.

At last she got up from her chair, her lips set with determination. She had to do something positive, or she would be in dire danger of 'giving way'—one of the cardinal sins as far as Aunt Jessie had been concerned. 'Och, she's a poor creature—always giving way,' had been her charitable aunt's ultimate condemnation of anyone who failed to face up to life with her own vigour and optimism.

But even positive action had its limits. She seemed faced with a choice between going to the cinema or washing her hair. In the end, the idea of warm water on her scalp seemed infinitely more appealing than the stuffy atmosphere of a cinema and, besides, it might help to banish the beginnings of the real headache that was threatening.

She was just towelling away the excess moisture when the doorbell went. 'Oh, no!' she muttered in disbelief. For a moment, she toyed with the idea of ignoring the summons, but she knew that whoever was waiting would have heard the radio playing and would know she was there, and as if to reinforce the realisation, the doorbell rang again, peremptorily. Catriona stifled a sigh as she trailed to answer it. At least this time it wouldn't be Jeremy, she thought as she flung open the door.

The breath left her throat in a little choking gasp as she looked into Jason's angry eyes. She tried to slam the door, but he was too quick for her. His hand closed bruisingly round her arm.

'Get dressed, Catriona,' he said. 'You're needed.'

'I'll do nothing of the sort.' She faced him defiantly. 'And how dare you burst in here like this without so much as a . . .'

'By your leave?' he finished for her, derisively. 'I'm sorry I haven't more time for the social niceties, but my errand is fairly urgent. Now, will you please get some clothes on and come with me.'

'Come where?'

'To the centre, of course.' He raised his eyebrows. 'The *ceilidh*'s in full swing—going a bomb too. Sal and her friends are doing you proud.'

'Then you don't need me.' She wrenched her arm free, glaring at him.

'How right you are,' he said, bitingly. 'As far as I'm personally concerned, you can stay in this little room and sulk until you rot. But there is someone who needs you— and it's for her sake I'm here.'

'Mitch?' she faltered.

'Clever girl.' He took her shoulder and propelled her in the direction of the bedroom door. 'Now, hurry.'

She hung back, resisting him. 'What's happened? You must tell me . . .'

'Nothing's happened. That's why we need you there,' he said. 'Your silent friend is sitting on the stairs at the centre. Milner—Miss Haydon, we've all been out in turn, trying to persuade her to come in and join us. Milner feels this could be a big break-through for the girl and I agree with him. But she won't budge—behaves as if she doesn't hear—so let's see what your powers of persuasion can do. You obviously feel that your approach with her is the right one, so we'll find out just how successful it is. That girl needs to be in the room with everyone else. She needs to be part of it. It's up to you to get her in there.'

'You're very altruistic all of a sudden,' she flashed, stung by his tone. 'And what do you need, Mr Lord? A spot of real-life drama to spice up your documentary? Will the cameras be on Mitch when she comes through the door?'

His lips were in a thin hard line. 'I've never hit a woman in my life,' he said coldly and precisely. 'But in your case I'm prepared to make an exception. I don't have to explain my motivation to you, but I will say this—filming is over for

157

the day, probably for good as far as the centre's concerned. We have as much as we need. Now move yourself, or I swear to God I'll dress you with my own hands.'

Catriona fled then, her hands clumsy and shaking as she opened the wardrobe door and fumbled amongst the clothes that hung there, grabbing the first thing that came to hand. Inevitably it was the violet skirt and the white silk blouse, and she stared at them stupidly for a moment, the memory of what had happened the last time she had attempted to wear them surging back into her brain. She flung them away across the bed as if they had bitten her and seized a pair of jeans and a dark roll-necked sweater. Her face was white as she stared at herself in the mirror, but she did nothing to alleviate her pallor with cosmetics. Her damp hair she scooped back into an elastic band, then she grabbed up her shoulder bag and walked out of the bedroom past Jason to the door.

He looked her over and his lip curled slightly. 'Party gear?' he asked evenly.

'Working clothes.' Her tone matched his.

They went down to the car in silence which was maintained as they drove to the centre.

The big hall was filled with shadows when they arrived and Catriona sensed rather than saw the slim figure sitting motionless on the bottom stair. She made her way to the other girl's side and sat down beside her. The sound of music and laughter from the sitting room was plainly audible, and Catriona knew by Mitch's rigidity that she was listening and aware. She put a hand lightly on her arm, expecting rejection, but it did not come.

'Enjoying the party?' She deliberately did not allow her voice to be too gentle. 'You've chosen a funny vantage point, I must say. It's draughty in this hall. Aren't you cold?'

She glimpsed the slight movement as Mitch shook her head.

'Well, I am.' Catriona pretended to shiver. 'And if I catch a chill, I shan't be able to sing—and they're all waiting for me.'

She felt she had struck the right note at last—the easy inconsequential tone that had characterised most of her one-sided conversations with the tense figure at her side.

She tried a little laugh. 'I'm nervous—isn't that stupid? But I am, just the same. It was easy singing at home. I knew everyone, and they were all friends. But I haven't many friends in London and I'm not used to singing to a room full of strangers. If I had a friend there it would be different.' She got up slowly, forcing herself to relax, not to betray her eagerness, the fact that her nervousness had nothing to do with the audience waiting for her in the sitting room. Almost casually, she reached her hand down to Mitch. 'Come and hear me sing,' she invited quietly. 'I shan't be nervous if you're there.'

It seemed like the longest moment of her life as she stood there with her hand outstretched, waiting. Even then, she could hardly believe it when Mitch's small cold hand closed round hers and together they walked through the dark hall to the sitting room door and the bright lights beyond it.

No one turned to look at them as they entered, Catriona registered with an inward sigh of relief. Unobtrusively, a space was made for them on one of the ancient, sagging sofas and they subsided on to it thankfully. Everyone seemed to be there—all the residents, Sally, Ian and some others she knew only as faces, and the entire television crew. They were all singing too—an uninhibited version of 'She'll be coming round the mountain' which everyone—especially the children—seemed to be enjoying.

But their arrival hadn't gone unnoticed. When the song ended and the laughter and applause died away, Catriona saw that Ian was on his feet and beckoning to her. After only a moment's hesitation she relinquished her grip on Mitch's hand and rose, threading her way through the people sitting on the floor to the front of the room.

'Well, she's come, people,' Ian called encouragingly to the room at last. 'Better late than never, I suppose!' He unslung his guitar and handed it to her with a wink and a smile. 'The floor is yours, sweetheart.'

Someone pushed a stool at her and Catriona hitched herself on to it, her mouth dry and her stomach churning.

'Here's one you all know,' she said, only the slightest quiver in her voice betraying her inner turmoil. 'The *Skye Boat Song.*'

They were all silent as she sang the refrain and launched into the verse, but under Ian's vigorous but silent encouragement they were all with her when the chorus came round again. 'Speed, bonny boat, like a bird on the wing—onward, the sailors cry.' The applause was tumultuous, dwarfing even her reception at Moira's party. She would have to sing again, she knew as she bowed a little stiffly from her perch. Automatically her eyes sought Mitch and she relaxed a little when she saw the girl was sitting there in the same place.

Encouraged, she sang the *Lewis Bridal Song* and followed it up with *Black is the Colour of my True Love's Hair*. Then, knowing that she had them in her grip, she put down the guitar and sang unaccompanied one of her own favourites, *She moved through the Fair*. She would have stopped then, but they wouldn't let her go.

'Come on, ducks.' That was Mrs Lamb. 'It's time these kids were in bed. Sing 'em a nice lullaby.'

Catriona's mind ran frantically over her repertoire as she picked up Ian's guitar again. She played a chord softly, hesitantly while she tried to make up her mind—and then she knew what she would sing. The chord had set off answering vibrations in her memory. It was a risk she was taking, she knew that, and it could go horribly wrong, but it was worth trying.

'My swan-song, then,' she announced, making herself

smile as if she didn't have a care in the world beyond pleasing them. '*The Eriskay Love Lilt.*'

Deliberately, she didn't look at Mitch as her fingers found the opening chords and her voice beguiled its way into the infinite charm and tenderness of the old Gaelic song. She saw Andrew sitting openly with Jean, his arm round her shoulders, draw her close as he recognised the melody—saw other faces echoing his smiling recognition round the room, and saw Jason, his face a dark, enigmatic mask leaning against the wall at the back of the room.

> 'When I'm lonely, dear white heart,
> Black the night, and wild the sea,
> By love's light, my foot finds
> The old pathway to thee . . .'

Everything—everyone else, including Mitch—was forgotten as the words came to her. She might have been alone with Jason in the big room. This time, she had no inhibitions. All the love, the wild longings he had aroused in her were in her voice. She gave herself to the melody as she wanted to give herself to him, and all the pain and rejection she had felt in the past weeks were contained in her words as she sang, 'Sad am I without thee.' She was so totally immersed in the emotion of the song she was creating, that she was oblivious to everything else.

The scream when it came cut shockingly across the melody, silencing her and sending her fingers sliding into discord. Mitch was on her feet, her hands twisting in agony, her eyes staring across the room into Catriona's.

'Mitch!' she cried again, and there was a world of desolation in the sound. 'Oh, Mitch!'

Catriona found herself thrusting the guitar at Ian. She thought afterwards she had probably trodden on people in her rush to be the first one at Mitch's side. Andrew, obviously shaken, was just getting to his feet.

She took the twisting hands, trying not to wince as they seized hers in an almost unbearable grip. She looked into

Mitch's face and spoke slowly and clearly.

'What's your name?'

'Carol—Carol Barton.' It was only a hoarse whisper, but Catriona's straining ears caught it.

'And who is Mitch?' She paused. 'Carol—who is Mitch?'

Carol's shoulders moved as if she was trying to shake off a burden suddenly grown too heavy for her to bear.

'He's dead,' she said dully. 'Oh God, he's dead.' And she began to cry with long, gulping sobs.

Andrew was there. 'Let's get her out of this crowd,' he said swiftly. 'You come too, Catriona. Jean, take her other arm.'

Gently but firmly the weeping girl was urged towards the door. Behind her, Catriona could hear Ian stepping into the breach, using his actor's skill to drag the crowd's attention back from what had just transpired. Before they had got into the hall, the singing had begun again, a little raggedly.

There was nothing very new in Carol's story, told there in the office while Jean made tea and rang the doctor. She had met Mitch at a pop concert in her home town eighteen months before. He was the guitarist with a group, but he had told her his ambition was to make it on his own as a serious folk singer. They were playing a number of gigs in neighbouring towns and she had followed the group around, just watching and listening to him. Eventually when they moved on, she went too. At first, everything was fine— Mitch even obtained a couple of solo bookings and was able to try out his folk act. But he didn't have the instant success he dreamed of. One booking agent told him frankly his value was as a group artist, not a soloist, and he became self-contained and morose.

'The group got rid of him in the end.' Carol clasped her hands round the warmth of her tea cup. 'He—he didn't want to know. Didn't rehearse—didn't try any more. They got sick. I couldn't blame them. He was so moody too, there was no living with him.'

It had been quite some time, she said, before she had realised the terrifying reason for these sudden changes in mood he seemed subject too. Even then, she hadn't really believed it. Not until she had found the hypodermic syringe hidden in a drawer. She had confronted him with it, begged him to get help, and he had promised that he would, but it was only the first of many such promises.

From then on Mitch's path had led downhill—fast, and Carol had been powerless to do anything to help him or prevent his eventual total disintegration.

'He couldn't get work,' she said. 'No one would touch him, because they didn't know how he was going to be. He wasn't getting any money and he needed money—for the stuff. I got a job in a supermarket, but that wasn't enough. It just paid our rent and food, and that wasn't what he needed. He used to come down to the supermarket and wait for me to finish work. One day he got sick of waiting. He hit this woman and grabbed her bag. They got him, of course, and he had to go to court. He got a suspended sentence and they said he had to get treatment. He said he would—he promised me.' Her mouth trembled uncontrollably. 'He said I kept on at him—that he couldn't stand it any longer, and he went. I didn't see him for nearly three weeks, then the police came for me.'

Mitch, she had discovered, was in hospital, but he was not receiving treatment. He had developed acute blood poisoning.

'I was there with him all the time,' she said. 'They couldn't do much for him. He was too far gone when they found him. I kept thinking—all the time—that if I hadn't kept on at him maybe he wouldn't have gone. Maybe he'd still be alive now. They said I could have his things—there wasn't much. He'd sold nearly everything to get money for the—stuff. But he'd always kept the guitar. He thought all the time that one day he was really going to make it. Having the guitar was like still having part of him.'

Andrew spoke gently. 'Where's the guitar now, Carol?'

She looked down dazedly as if she expected to find it in its usual place, cradled in her arms. Her shoulders moved again wearily. 'It's upstairs—I think.'

'Do you want it?' Jean bent over her, her warm face compassionate.

There was a long silence, then Carol shook her head. 'No,' she said simply. 'Not any more.'

The doctor's arrival relieved Catriona from her vigil. All during the pitiful recital she had knelt at Carol's feet, her hands clutched in that fierce grip. Now she moved stiffly back into the dark hall, rubbing her finger-joints. The singing was still going on, but she could not face a crowd yet. She went down the passage to the kitchen and poured herself a glass of water.

From behind her Jason said quietly, 'All right?'

'Yes.' She made herself speak normally. 'The doctor's with her now.'

'I meant you,' he said abruptly.

Catriona gave a slight shake of her head and took another sip from her glass.

He came over and stood looking down at her. 'I shouldn't have made you come here tonight. I'm sorry,' he said.

'I'm not.' She looked up at him gravely. 'She's talked and told us everything. Now Andrew can get help for her. Besides, I knew what I might be doing. I knew that song meant something to her and I used it deliberately.'

His eyes were hard. 'I didn't get that impression. It seemed to me you were singing from your heart.'

She was silent. He was the last person she could tell that every word, every note of music had ached with her wanting him.

'Poor Catriona!' There was an odd note in his voice. 'Always fated to fall in love with the wrong man.'

He knew. The humiliating awareness kept her eyes fixed

164

on the floor. She couldn't face him and see—what? Mockery? Pity? Sudden tension invaded her body as Jason reached out and drew her to him, holding her against him with unwonted gentleness.

His hand came up and stroked her face, then found her chin, lifting it with firm insistence. He was going to kiss her, and then her self-betrayal would be complete. With a strength she had not known she possessed, she dragged herself out of his arms and stared at him, masking her other emotions with anger.

'Save your compassion, Mr Lord.' She hated herself for sounding so young and breathless. 'Keep it for people like Carol. She needs it. I—I don't.'

There was a loaded pause. Then, 'As you wish,' he said, his voice flat and cold, and left her.

CHAPTER EIGHT

IT seemed strange to come to work and find the Home Counties' TV vans gone from the road outside the centre. Strange too to find how the whole crew was missed, especially by the people who had complained most vociferously at the beginning of filming about the invasion of their privacy. Catriona listened and smiled and agreed, and kept her own heartache strictly to herself.

'My, that Mr Lord was a dish!' Mrs Lamb smacked her lips reminiscently as she loaded the last article of laundry into the elderly spin dryer and closed its lid. 'If I was a young bit of a thing like you, Catriona, I'd have been after him like a shot.'

165

'Girls these days don't know when they're on to a good thing,' Mrs Waters, one of the newer residents, remarked enviously.

Catriona, intercepting an anxious look from Jean, made herself smile. 'Oh, I think we do,' she said with an attempt at lightness. 'It's the thought of all the competition that we find a bit daunting.'

'Hmm.' Mrs Lamb set the drier going. 'Well, I think if a thing's worth having, it's worth fighting for. Maybe if I'd fought a bit harder, Bert wouldn't have gone off like that. But there again, he probably would have. Law unto himself, is my Bert. Always was.'

'She sounds as if she would be quite ready to have him back in spite of the way he left her,' Catriona told Jean when they were alone.

Jean smiled a little. 'I don't doubt it. That's one of the things Andrew and I have always noticed—one of the encouraging things—that people don't simply write off relationships which have gone wrong, even when to outsiders they seem a total disaster. You hear girls with black eyes and broken ribs making excuses for the husbands who gave them to them.' She sighed. 'I don't think I possess that sort of courage—or optimism.'

Catriona shook her head. 'Nor me.' She paused. 'How's Mitch—I mean Carol—today?'

'Very calm, very rational. She's seeing Dr Winters this morning, and she's given Andrew her parents' address in the north. He's going to write to them to see what the chances are of her going back there for a while at least. It seems there was a terrible row when she left originally, and she's afraid they may not want her back. I hope she's wrong. Affection and a stable background are just what she needs at the moment.'

Andrew appeared in the doorway, looking harassed. 'Mrs Henderson,' he mouthed. 'On the warpath too, I'm afraid. Could we have some coffee?'

166

Mrs Henderson's mood seemed no sweeter when Catriona carried the tray into the office. She acknowledged her quiet greeting with a sniff and turned immediately back to Andrew.

'As I was saying, Mr Milner, I can see no useful purpose being served by these people becoming part of the studio audience. If I had been consulted, I would have said so.'

'I'm sorry you feel like that, Mrs Henderson.' Andrew tried to be conciliatory. 'But I don't see any harm in it. After all, they did take part in the documentary and it will be their only chance to see the programme. We have no television set here, as you know. And it's Mr Lord's intention that the residents should take part in the studio discussion.'

Mrs Henderson snorted. 'Mr Lord has a deplorably high-handed attitude,' she said. 'I think he has lost sight of the fact that these people are charity cases.'

'I think Mr Lord knows precisely what these people are,' Andrew said quietly. 'I also think he knows precisely how to run his programme. It's hardly our place to dictate its format or say how the studio audience should be constituted.'

'Well, I am extremely disappointed in the whole thing,' Mrs Henderson announced. 'I wish I had never given permission for the filming. I'm not at all sure that I shouldn't forbid the programme to be shown.'

'I think it's a little late for that,' Andrew said drily. 'It's scheduled to go out on Monday evening. Besides, surely any cancellation of the project would have to be a Trust decision, and I doubt whether a meeting of all the trustees could be convened in time.'

Mrs Henderson glared at him, and remained silent.

After a pause, Andrew went on, 'I must say there seems to be an amazing amount of interest in the programme from other sources. I've been asked to take part in a radio forum on the problems of the homeless, and one of the evening

167

papers was on the phone earlier asking about us and our work.'

'Indeed?' she snapped. 'I hope all this publicity has the desired effect and does not simply make people discontented and ungrateful. I have grave doubts about the wisdom of the whole undertaking. Good day, Mr Milner.'

'I was afraid of that,' Andrew said gloomily, after Mrs Henderson had gone. 'I was hoping she wouldn't find out that everyone from the centre was going to be in the audience. Let's just hope she doesn't refer to them in public as charity cases, or there could be a riot.'

'Perhaps that's what this place needs,' Catriona muttered. 'Well, not a riot, but some kind of shake-up among the trustees. They can't all have her rigid attitude, surely.'

'On the contrary. I think there are several who would like to have a more positive say in running things, but no one wants to make the first move—because she's James Henderson's widow and it's Henderson money that has been involved up to now. It's understandable, I suppose—loyalty to the name and all that, but it would be easier for the centre if she had rather less control.'

Sally was sympathetic when Catriona recounted the day's events over supper that night.

'Money's the answer, of course,' she said. 'If the trust was bolstered up by outside finance, then Mrs H. could be ushered out of the driving seat.'

Catriona nodded rather unhappily. 'It seems cruel, but she's so—hostile towards the centre and everything Andrew is trying to do. Anything she does comes from a sense of duty, not from any real interest in people. I can't believe she's the right person to be at the head of a charity organisation.'

Sally nodded sombrely. 'In her heart, she might be quite glad to be relieved of the job,' she said. She paused, then grinned at Catriona. 'How about a demo at the studio on

Monday night—banners with "Henderson must Go" on them? Think she'd take the hint?'

Catriona smiled reluctantly. 'I doubt it. She'd probably close the centre instead.'

'It's a big week for all of us on television,' Sally remarked as they cleared away. 'The centre documentary on Monday, and the play on Wednesday. Can't offer you a seat in the studio for *Under the Skin*, I'm afraid.'

Catriona shook her head. 'I'm—I'm not going to the studio for *Here and Now* either,' she said constrainedly, and saw Sally's eyebrows shoot up.

'Why in the world not?' she exclaimed. 'You and Jason aren't still carrying on this weird feud of yours, surely?'

Catriona avoided her glance. 'That's one way of putting it, I suppose.'

'I could think of others.' Sally was silent for a moment, biting her lip. 'Love, you frighten me sometimes, you really do. Jeremy was bad enough—but Jason!'

'You have no need to worry,' Catriona said steadily. 'I don't have any illusions about his—kindness to me.'

'Does he know how you feel about him?' Sally demanded, and Catriona nodded slowly.

'Oh dear.' Sally turned on the taps in the sink with unnecessary violence. 'That wasn't a very clever move.'

Catriona sighed. 'I know that, but I didn't tell him. He—guessed.'

Sally sniffed. 'How perceptive of him. And what now? One of those brief spectacular affairs he's so good at? At least it might get him out of your system.'

There was a constriction in Catriona's throat. 'I don't think it would—somehow.'

She lay awake for a long time that night, looking into a future that became progressively more bleak and forlorn as she examined it. There was, of course, no earthly reason why her path and Jason's should ever cross again, she thought

169

drearily. He would not be coming to the centre again, and she would stay away from the television studios. Sally was now the only real link between them and she would soon be going off on tour.

An old and cynical saying came drifting back into her mind. 'Love makes time pass; time makes love pass.' She wondered achingly if it was true.

Julie moved into the flat over the weekend and Catriona was able to push her own problems to the back of her mind in the uproar of re-organising the furniture and drawer space to accommodate Julie's belongings and generally making her feel at home.

Catriona had not told Andrew that she was not going to the television centre with the rest of them, but when the subject did come up on Monday afternoon, he accepted her decision without comment. But she felt he was disappointed in her all the same.

She was just typing the last of the letters he had given her earlier when rapid footsteps sounded outside, and Mrs Henderson marched in. She was carrying a folded newspaper under one arm and there were bright spots of colour burning in both cheeks. She ignored Andrew completely, fixing her inimical gaze on Catriona.

'You're dismissed, Miss Muir,' she said. 'Please go at once, and understand that I shall be writing to Miss Shaw about her conduct in recommending a person of your moral character to work for a Christian organisation.'

'Mrs Henderson!' Andrew was on his feet. 'You have no right . . .'

'No right?' Mrs Henderson turned on him, her eyes blazing. 'When she drags the name of the Trust in the mire along with her own?'

'Please, Mrs Henderson,' Catriona was ashamed to find her voice was shaking, 'you must tell me what I've done.'

'You play the innocent very well, miss. You took in Mr Milner, but I never trusted you from the first. Collect your

170

things together and go. I shall wait here until you're safely off the premises.'

'Mrs Henderson,' Andrew interposed himself between them, 'I insist that you tell me what Catriona has done to deserve this—tirade. I must warn you there is such a thing as slander.'

Mrs Henderson tossed the paper she was carrying on to the table in front of him. 'Look for yourself,' she said.

His face bewildered and angry, he began to read and Catriona saw the anger turn to embarrassment and his eyes glance up at her swiftly, almost accusingly.

'Andrew, what is it?' she begged.

He held out the paper in silence. It was a gossip column, she saw that at a glance—items about various celebrities interspersed with pictures. One of the pictures looked oddly familiar—a dark-haired girl standing clutching a pillow. Amazed, she stared at it more closely.

'But that's me!' she exclaimed. Puzzled, her eye travelled on and she saw the caption underneath.

'Pretty Scots songbird Catriona Muir has found a comfortable nest in the flat of TV producer Jason Lord. But this talented twenty-year-old isn't there just to sing sweet lullabies. She lists the domestic arts—bedmaking in particular—among her many capabilities.

'Housekeeping for the much-sought-after Mr Lord doesn't fill her days, however. When she's finished smoothing his pillows, she's to be found working for the Henderson Trust—a hostel for the homeless.

'Which could explain why Mr Lord's prestigious *Here and Now* programme tonight is taking the lid off this rather lowly charity.

'Charity—as Mr Lord and his lovely *au pair* would no doubt agree—certainly begins at home.'

Catriona put the paper down slowly and stood there, feeling sick. She hadn't needed to read the name at the end of the column to realise who had written this farrago of distortion and insinuation. How in the world could she have forgotten? she asked herself despairingly, recalling the loaded conversation she had only partly understood in the television cafeteria and Roger Hunt's visit to Jason's flat. She had intended to tell Jason about it, but subsequent happenings had driven it out of her head.

'It was the *Globe* that rang me the other day,' Andrew said flatly. 'I wondered how they knew so much about us.'

She looked up at him. 'You don't believe this?'

'You're trying to say this reporter is lying?' Mrs Henderson rapped. 'Where were you, may I ask, when that picture was taken? Was it in fact Jason Lord's bedroom?'

'Yes,' Catriona nodded unhappily. 'But it isn't what you think. I—I don't live with Jason. I share a flat with Sally Fenton. She's an actress—you can ask her . . .'

'An actress!' Mrs Henderson filled the word with venom. 'And also a friend of Mr Lord's, I have no doubt.'

'Yes, she is, but I don't see . . .'

'And can you swear to me that you have never——' Mrs Henderson hesitated—'spent the night at Mr Lord's home?'

'I did once, but . . .'

'You see!' Mrs Henderson turned to Andrew, spreading her hands triumphantly. 'She has the effrontery to admit it!'

'Her private life is her own affair,' he said quietly.

'Certainly, while it remains private. But Miss Muir has allowed it to become public property and has dared to involve the name of the Trust in her sordid intrigues. I repeat, Mr Milner, she must go.'

Andrew stood up very straight. 'Understand this, Mrs Henderson. Sack Catriona and Miss Haydon and I will leave as well. I don't believe one word of this distasteful piece of garbage. I agree it's unfortunate that the name of the Trust should have been dragged in . . .'

'My name too, Mr Milner.'

'But Catriona is not to blame for that,' he continued as if

172

she had not spoken. 'I can't imagine this was printed with her knowledge or consent.'

'If you and Miss Haydon do anything so ill-judged, Mr Milner, I shall close the centre down.' Mrs Henderson spoke with cold finality.

'Oh, no.' Catriona could bear no more. 'Andrew, you mustn't! These people need you. I can get another job. She can't sack me anyway, because I—I resign. I couldn't stay, knowing how Mrs Henderson regards me.'

She picked up her handbag with trembling hands.

'I think that is probably the most satisfactory solution.' Mrs Henderson sat down. 'Mr Milner will arrange for a week's wages to be sent to you.'

Catriona shook her head. 'That won't be necessary.' She tried to smile at Andrew's concerned face. 'Goodbye, Andrew. Please say goodbye to Jean and the others for me.'

'This isn't the end of it, Catriona.' He took her hand. 'I'll be in touch.'

It wasn't until Catriona was on her way back to the flat that she realised she still carried Mrs Henderson's copy of the *Globe*. Sitting in the tube, she unfolded it and re-read the offending piece. She felt as if she had been kicked. Surely there must be some comeback against this kind of outrageous gossip, she told herself vehemently, but her defiance wilted when she studied the photograph. It was such a damning piece of evidence. And she had told Roger Hunt that she was doing Jason's housework. But where had he got the other details—the fact that she sang—the Trust? All the facts stated in the piece were correct. Her only complaint could be in the way they were represented, but even here she was not sure of her ground.

The train started off again with a jerk and Catriona leaned back in her seat, closing her eyes wearily. Her only comfort was that so few people knew her in London. But the same could not be said for Jason. Her eyes flew open, and hot colour flooded her face as the realisation burst upon her.

She had been solely concerned with the article's effect upon herself. She had not stopped to consider that she was not the only person involved. Had he seen the column? she wondered frantically. He would know, if anyone did, whether anything could be done to put the record straight.

She got out at the next station and found a telephone booth. She got through to Home Counties Television and was put through to Jason's office. But it was Diane who answered. Mr Lord, she was told, had left for home some time before.

Catriona left the Underground and hailed a passing taxi to take her to Belmont Gardens. They were already pulling into the little square before the first doubts about the wisdom of her action began to creep into her mind, but she put them firmly to one side as she paid the driver. She was to blame, she knew that. She had talked to the reporter and allowed a photographer into his flat. Jason was entitled to an explanation at least.

She bit her lip as she ran up the steps to the gleaming front door and pressed the bell long and hard. Her heart was beating unmercifully as she stood there, willing Jason to be at home, to answer the door.

At last, the door opened.

'What do you want?' The harshness in his voice was worse than she could have imagined.

'Please let me in.' Her voice was pleading, breathless. 'I must see you—tell you . . .' She held out the crumpled copy of the *Globe* under his icily contemptuous gaze. He was turning away. He wasn't going to let her speak. With all her strength, Catriona threw herself against the closing door, pushing past him into the hall. There she faced him, her eyes dark with trouble, trying to control her hurried breathing and calm herself sufficiently to speak.

For a terrified moment, she thought Jason was going to forcibly eject her from the house. Then, with a shrug, he opened the lounge door and ironically bowed her towards it.

The first thing she saw was the *Globe*, open at the gossip page, flung down on the sofa. She swung towards him.

'You must let me tell you how it was.'

'Explanations aren't necessary,' he said with a kind of controlled violence. 'Whatever twisted little reasons you may have had for this—hatchet job on my privacy, they must have seemed good to you at the time. Nothing else matters.'

'But it does,' she insisted, and to her horror, her vision blurred and misted.

'Oh, God!' He spoke with disgusted weariness. 'Every trick in the book! How many times have I got to tell you that tears don't work with me?'

'I'm not going to cry.' Catriona thrust back the tears and her chin came up with some of its old defiance. 'But you won't listen to me, and you must.'

He threw himself into a chair and stared at her, his eyes hard and inimical. 'You have my undivided attention.'

So she told him about it—her meeting with Roger Hunt, and his arrival at the flat while she was doing the housework, all the misgivings she had felt at the time.

'Then—afterwards, it went completely out of my head.' She did not dare to look at him, to remind him of the events which had wiped everything else from her memory. 'I suppose he must have started to find out about the Trust—and when he discovered I worked there, it must have—jogged his memory. So he wrote this.'

There was a long silence. Then, 'What kind of a fool do you take me for?' Jason demanded, and Catriona shrank at the menace in his voice. 'Didn't it occur to you that if you'd told me at the beginning I might have been able to put a stop to it before it even started?'

'I—I did try to contact you . . .'

'So you said. What was to stop you telling Diane, my

175

secretary? She's perfectly capable of putting the skids under Hunt and his breed. That's one of the things she's paid for.'

'I didn't think of that.'

'You didn't think!' he lashed her. 'Oh, you thought all right. I could even have put the idea into your head. I said it would be the perfect revenge if you told everyone I was Jon Lisle. But I didn't bargain for this—slime of lies and innuendo. What possessed you to tell them all this? Surely not more publicity for that beloved centre of yours? I don't think they'll thank you for this sort anyway.'

'I've got the sack,' Catriona said tightly. 'That's one reason why I came here. I thought if I explained to you how it happened, you might talk to Mrs Henderson—convince her it isn't true.'

'The next time I speak to Mrs Henderson will be on the air tonight,' he said. 'What happened? Didn't the stalwart Andrew speak up for you, or did he back hastily away when he found the goods were second-hand?'

She looked at him bewilderedly. 'That's a cruel thing to say!'

'Perhaps. Is that why you prefer well-meaning ineffectuals like Andrew?' He flung up a hand to stop the protest already forming on her lips. 'Oh yes, Catriona, he is ineffectual or he could have sorted out Alice Henderson a long time ago. He has the majority of the other trustees on his side already. All he needed was to push a little. He's a nice guy, but he needs someone else to do his dirty work for him. Do you see that as your future role?'

'I've told you, I've got the sack,' she said, her mouth trembling in spite of herself.

He laughed angrily. 'I suppose you'd forgotten that malice has a nasty way of backfiring. God! I knew I'd made you angry at times—but this! What in hell made you do it? You can't still be angry with me over the Jeremy business, surely?'

176

'No.' Catriona shook her head dazedly. Jeremy seemed to be part of another world, a different existence.

'Then didn't it occur to you that labelling yourself as my mistress would hurt no one but yourself? I've never claimed to live like a saint, after all, but you . . . even when I was holding you, I would have sworn you were innocent.'

He stopped abruptly and rose from his chair, his eyes narrowing as if a new and not particularly palatable thought had come to him. For a moment he stood in silence, staring at her until she felt naked under his bleak, abrasive glance.

Then he laughed, softly and without amusement. The laugh chilled Catriona more than his previous anger and she stepped back as he came towards her.

'So that was it,' he said, his voice too pleasant. 'I took no for an answer, didn't I, Catriona, when all the time you really wanted to say yes. How thoughtless of me not to have been more persuasive! Perhaps you aren't the innocent you seemed, but you played the part too well, darling. I apologise for being taken in.'

He was reaching for her and she braced her hands, trying to push him away from her. 'No—Jason. Please! You're wrong. I . . .'

'I think we'll forget the word "no".' She was no match for his strength as he pulled her against him. His mouth, sensually persuasive, teased the lobe of her ear. 'Poor little Catriona! All that wishful thinking, and I really had no idea. I was convinced you were saving yourself for marriage and the well-meaning Andrew, but if it was really my bed you wanted all the time, darling, you only had to drop me a hint in private. There was no need to take a half-page ad in a newspaper.'

Catriona was shaking as if she stood in a high wind. His words seemed to sear against her skin, now tinglingly alive under his caressing mouth.

'Jason, you—we mustn't . . .'

177

'Why not?' He lifted her in his arms and was striding with her to the door. 'You invented the fiction. Why shouldn't I make it fact?'

She kicked and struggled all the way to his room, but he took no more notice than if she had been a troublesome child. He kicked the door closed behind them and carried her to the bed, dropping her almost negligently into the centre of that luxurious black and silver quilt. 'What a pity I'd already made the bed. But you can always make it again afterwards. You did say that was your particular—forte?'

She gave a little protesting cry, but it was smothered under the merciless pressure of his mouth. She could fight no more. All she could do was lie rigid in his embrace and show him that he was wrong. That she didn't want him . . .

It was a silent battle and over almost as soon as it had begun. Catriona's head was still whispering 'No' even as her body melted under his expert hands. It was her own urgency, her own desire she could no longer deny. She was returning his kisses, her trembling body acknowledging his mastery.

At last, he took his lips from hers and sat up. She watched him, her eyes widening endlessly as he pulled off his tie and threw it to the floor beside the bed, then began to unbutton his shirt, tugging it free from his close-fitting grey denim pants.

'Touch me, Catriona.' His voice might be soft, but it was a command, not a request.

Very tentatively she sat up, until she was half kneeling beside him, then slipped her hands inside his open shirt. His skin was warm and smooth and the rapid beat of his heart under her fingertips seemed to echo the thunder of her own clamouring pulses. Suddenly shy, she paused, but his hands came up instantly, capturing hers and holding them against his body.

He half groaned her name, propelling her back against the pillows, his lips seeking hers with a demand that scared and exalted her at the same time. Catriona lost all sense of time as she lay there in his arms. Right and wrong had no meaning any more in a world where the only reality was the weight of his body, vibrant in its masculinity, against hers. Every nerve ending, every pulse in her body was asking a question for which Jason alone had the answer.

Then, suddenly, she was alone. For a moment she lay there bewildered, then she felt her cheeks grow hot as she realised he must have left her to finish undressing. But at last the silence in the room unnerved her and she lifted herself on to her elbow and looked for him. He was standing staring out of the window, his back turned to her, but he must have heard her movement because he turned.

'Jason?' Her voice shook a little as she stretched out her hand, willing him to come back to her.

He walked to the bed and stood looking down at her, ignoring her outstretched hand.

'You'd better get dressed,' he said curtly.

She glanced down at herself, crimsoning as she realised for the first time the disarray his seeking hands had created, then her eyes sought his, dismayed, as she took in what he had said.

'Jason—what's wrong?' All her longing for him echoed in the pitiful little query.

He gave a mirthless laugh. 'Just about everything, I'd say. Or wouldn't you agree?'

She bent her head. 'Was it me?' she asked in a low voice. 'Did I do something wrong? I didn't know . . .'

'No!' His violence startled her. 'Dear God, if you only knew . . .' He shook his head. 'It's not anything you did, Catriona. It's what you are.'

She was dragging her clothing together, fumbling with the fastenings with hands that shook. 'And what am I?' she appealed to him on the verge of tears.

His eyes held hers. 'You're what I thought originally,' he said quietly. 'I know now—it isn't a pretence, all that innocence. It's real because you're still a virgin.'

179

'And that makes a difference?' She tried hard to smile, but it was a failure.

'It does to me,' he said sombrely. 'For one thing, it imposes limitations which I don't feel inclined to accept right now. But there are other—less selfish reasons why I should get you out of here before any real harm is done.'

'Is all this supposed to stop me wanting you?' she asked in a low voice.

'I made you want me.' His voice was equally quiet. 'I brought you here because I was angry, and that's why I'm telling you to go. A girl should be taken in love, not anger—especially the first time.'

She wanted to tell him that she had love enough to cover his anger and her jealousy of Moira, and every other emotion that could conceivably keep them from each other, but the tears were salt on her lips and the words would not come.

Jason's eyes looked broodingly down on her. 'You'll thank me one day. Passion doesn't heal wounds, you know. It simply opens deeper ones. One day you'll meet a man you can—care for in all the ways there are, and you'll be able to give yourself to him without regrets.' He walked to the door. 'I'll get you a taxi.'

By the time it was at the door, Catriona had regained some measure of self-control. It took all the remnants of her pride to walk past him in the hall as he held the door open for her.

Quietly and without a backward glance she went down the steps, got into the cab and gave the driver her address.

As the taxi pulled away, it passed another car which was just entering the square. Catriona looked back for one last, hungry glimpse of him and saw that the car had stopped in front of the flat. The occupant got out and ran up the steps to the open door where Jason was waiting. She was wearing black with a wide, floating cape and her red-gold hair gleamed in the late sunlight. Sick at heart, Catriona watched

180

Moira Dane go into Jason's arms before the door shut, closing them in together.

It had been raining for most of the day, a soft persistent drizzle which seemed to penetrate even the most waterproof of clothing. Catriona sat by the fire in Mrs McGregor's kitchen re-reading Sally's letter.

Ten days had passed since her precipitate flight from London back to Torvaig and the refuge it seemed to offer. But she had deceived herself, she thought, staring across the homely room to the streaming window. There was no solace for her here. In fact the torment of her feelings for Jason seemed somehow intensified by the very remoteness of the village and the lack of diversion.

She had had no very clear idea of what she was going to do in Torvaig when she had left that morning, bringing the bare essentials with her in the old rucksack. Her clothes and other possessions she had accumulated, even her guitar, were still at the flat, and she had written to Sally, enclosing some money and asking her to have them sent on. She had thought vaguely that she might stay at Muir House, that perhaps Mrs Mackintosh might accommodate her for a while in return for some help with the housework, but she was soon disabused of that notion. Business was not brisk enough for that, Mrs Mackintosh had told her, her thin mouth set in lines of discontent. She had bought Muir House as a going concern, but she felt she had been sadly deceived. If things didn't pick up soon, they were going to put the place back on the market and away back to Glasgow.

Catriona had almost been ashamed to present herself at Mrs McGregor's door, but the warmth of her welcome had overwhelmed her. She had been drawn inside, presented with a large cup of steaming tea, clucked and exclaimed over, and then driven upstairs inexorably to the tiny spare room with its narrow bed. With amazing tact, Mrs McGregor had ignored the dark shadows under her unexpected

181

guest's wistful eyes, and her patently ringless hands. She simply behaved as if the time in London had been a temporary aberration from which Catriona was now, mercifully, recovered.

She sent her out for long walks over the hills and along the shore, filled her plate with wholesome food, and waved a dismissive hand at Catriona's insistence that she must leave and find herself a job in Glasgow, maybe, or Inverness.

'Och, there's no hurry. No hurry at all,' was all she would say.

But she would have to find something to do soon, Catriona thought. Sally's letter had made her feel restless, an all-too-potent reminder of the world she had left behind.

Sally had been incredibly kind that night, she thought. When she realised that Catriona was determined to catch the first train back to Scotland the next day, she had not attempted to argue with her any more or ask any disturbing questions. And both she and Julie had restrained their curiosity nobly over the article in the *Globe*.

She could not bring herself to watch the television programme about the centre. She had pleaded the necessity of an early night with the long journey ahead of her and gone to bed, only to lie awake, her ears straining to catch any sound from the sitting room where Julie and Sally were watching it. She had pretended to be asleep when they eventually came quietly into the bedroom. Sally's whispered remark had come clearly to her ears, however.

'I felt quite sorry for that woman, in spite of the awful things she said about the people at the centre. She was absolutely destroyed. I don't think she even knew what was happening to her.'

According to Sally's letter, things were changing rapidly at the centre. Following the programme, Mrs Henderson had resigned her position on the board of trustees, and a new trust was being worked out to include representatives of several large charitable foundations which had come forward with offers of financial help. Andrew and Jean were being married in a fortnight's time, the letter continued on a more personal note, and Carol Barton's parents had come to take her home with them.

'And I have orders to tell you that Mrs Lamb's Bert has turned up,' wrote Sally. 'Apparently he saw the programme on television and decided he missed her and the children. He's working in Manchester, so they're all off there.

'I don't suppose you saw *Under the Skin*, but it was very well received by the critics, and Hugo is producing Jason's new one early in the autumn. There's a rumour that Jason may give up his documentary work to devote himself to play-writing, but he's pretty tight-lipped about the whole thing.'

Catriona folded the sheets of paper and replaced them in the envelope with a stifled sigh. If Jason did decide to become a full-time playwright, at least he would have a ready-made leading lady, she thought bitterly.

The rain petered out towards evening and Catriona, tugging on a thick sweater over her shirt and jeans to counteract the chilly breeze which had sprung up, decided to go for a walk along the shore before supper.

The clouds had lifted over the western horizon and the sun was sinking in a blaze of baleful red. She wandered down to the water's edge and stood for a long time looking out at the dark shapes of the islands. The softly creaming water lapped within inches of her sandalled feet and a swooping gull cried out, a harsh melancholy sound that made her shiver and turn away. This had been her home for most of her life, but suddenly she felt alien and alone. She walked back up the beach and paused, surprised. A man's dark figure was standing on the grass verge of the shore road. Her first thought was that it must be a stranger because he did not wave or call to her as any of the local men would have done. Then the first tingle of awareness began to slide over her skin.

She halted abruptly, staring towards him, her eyes wide and incredulous in her startled face. As if in answer to her hesitation, he himself moved, jumping down on to the rock-strewn sand and striding towards her. When he was only a couple of feet away from her, he stopped.

'Hello, Catriona,' he said, unsmilingly.

'Jason?' There was still disbelief in her voice. She began to tremble. 'What are you doing here?'

'Sally asked me to bring your things from London.'

Whatever she had expected him to say, it wasn't that.

'I see,' she said helplessly, after a moment's pause. 'Then you're on holiday—or something.'

'Something,' he agreed. His voice was quite pleasant, but his grey eyes held hers with a relentless unswerving gaze.

Her hands twisted together. 'You've chosen an out-of-the-way place.'

'The choice wasn't mine, Catriona.' She looked at him, a question in her eyes and he took a swift step towards her, his tone roughening. 'Dear God, do I have to spell it out for you?'

'Yes.' There was a sudden bubble of exultant joy rising inside her. 'Yes, Jason, I think you do.'

'I'm here because it's where you are—because that's where I must be. And if you run away from me again, I'll still come after you, and I'll keep coming until I've won you and taught you not to be afraid any more—of me, of life or anything else.'

'I'm not afraid,' she whispered. The joy was showing on her face now, trembling in her smile, shining from her eyes. 'And I'm yours if you want me, Jason. I—I always have been.'

He lifted her in a fierce embrace almost off her feet, holding her against him for a long moment before his mouth found hers. When he released her they were both breathless. He placed his hands under her chin and lifted her face to his with rough tenderness.

184

'Now tell me why the hell you ran away from me? I couldn't believe it the next day when Sal said you'd gone. I had my wooing all planned—flowers, theatre tickets, dinners for two—even down to the special licence burning a hole in my pocket at this moment.'

She said, faltering a little, 'A—licence? You want to— marry me?'

'What else?' he said with devastating simplicity. He bent and brushed her mouth lightly with his. His smile teased her. 'What other solution is there? All my efforts at seduction have gone sadly awry. I hope I have better fortune on our wedding night.'

She flushed, and buried her face in his shirt with a little incoherent murmur.

'That had better be an acceptance of my proposal.' His hand stroked her hair. His voice held a tremor of laughter. 'I think a twenty-four-hour engagement is about all I can stand.'

Catriona kept her head resolutely bent. 'Jason, what about Moira?'

'That was over a long time ago,' he said abruptly. 'I still saw her from time to time, but she was only part of the defence I was trying to build against you.'

She glanced at him swiftly. 'But she came to the flat that day—as I was leaving.'

'So she did,' he agreed calmly. 'She'd been having a long and liquid lunch with Hugo and he'd told her he was doing my new play. She'd come round to see if there was a part for her. She soon lost interest in me when she found there wasn't. She told me something else too—she was responsible for that damned piece in the *Globe*. Hunt would probably never have bothered to write it, but she chivvied him into it.'

'But why did she do that?'

'Because she knew I would hate it,' he said frankly. 'We were—quite close for a time, and I think she felt we could be again. But you spelled danger, so she picked the best way

185

she could think of to kill any relationship we might have stone dead.'

'But when you left me—after her party, you went back to her then.'

'I went back to the party,' he corrected. 'But not for Moira's sake. My executive producer and a couple of others were there and I wanted to talk over the idea of featuring the Henderson Trust on *Here and Now*. It meant reorganising some schedules, so I had to work fast.' He kissed her again. 'So you were jealous of Moira, were you? Excellent! Now you know what I went through.'

'You couldn't have been jealous of Jeremy,' she said slowly. 'Right from the start, you knew that would never work.'

'I wasn't thinking of Jeremy,' he said. 'I thought you were falling in love with Andrew Milner.'

'Andrew?' She gazed at him, frankly incredulous. 'But he loves Jean . . .'

'I knew that too. I was so afraid for you, my darling, so convinced that you were going to eat out your heart for the wrong man all over again.'

'I thought you were sorry for me because you'd guessed I was in love with you,' she whispered.

'No,' he said. 'I never guessed that. I was so tied up with trying to fight my own feelings, I completely misread the whole situation. But after I tried to make love to you at the flat that afternoon, I knew that I could never be satisfied with just an affair. I knew then that I wanted you with me always—as my wife. The only thing I wasn't sure of was if I could make you want me as a husband. I'm a bad-tempered devil and I like my own way. The only thing I can say in my own favour is that I love you.'

'That's more than enough.' She smiled up at him and he bent, swiftly pressing his mouth to the tip-tilted corners of her lips.

'It was Sal who put me on the right track,' he said. 'I went

186

round to the flat and demanded to know where you'd gone. I let her see I'd shake it out of her if I had to. Instead she calmly handed me this piece of paper with your address on it and said that as long as I was coming to find you, I might as well deliver your clothes to you as well. She said it would save having to buy a trousseau.' He grinned reminiscently. 'I think my jaw must have dropped, because she hit me— quite hard, and called me a blind, selfish idiot, among other things.'

'And where are my clothes?' Catriona demanded.

'In the boot of my car.' He rubbed his chin ruefully. 'It's parked along the road. I still haven't the faintest idea where I'm going to spend the night.'

She hesitated. 'Well, I daresay Mrs McGregor would find you a corner.'

'Is that where you're staying?' he asked and, when she nodded, gave a swift headshake. 'No, my darling, I prefer to remain safely at a distance until we're married. I'm not sharing a roof with you until I also have the right to share your bed.'

'We-ell—' her eyes danced suddenly, 'there's always Muir House. Mrs Mackintosh would be delighted, I know. But you must come back with me now, Jason. Mrs McGregor would never forgive me if I didn't bring you back to supper.'

'I think I can trust myself for that long,' he said drily. He pulled her against him hard, making her totally aware of his need for her. His kiss was long and deep, just within the bounds of self-control. 'Oh, darling,' he said huskily, 'if you have any mercy at all, don't keep me waiting much longer.'

Mrs McGregor was sitting by the fire when they came in, and she glanced up from the mail order catalogue she was reading.

'Well now, Catriona.' The situation was assessed in one twinkling look. 'So this is your man.'

'Yes,' said Catriona.

Best Seller Romances

Romances you have loved

Mills & Boon Best Seller Romances are the love stories that have proved particularly popular with our readers. They really are "back by popular demand." These are the other titles to look out for this month.

WILD MELODY
by Sara Craven

On the strength of a brief holiday romance with Jeremy Lord, Catriona left her quiet Scottish home and came up to London to marry him. But Jeremy, of course, had forgotten all about her by now – and instead she found herself involved with his sophisticated uncle Jason. Who was even more out of her league than Jeremy had been . . .

BLUEGRASS KING
by Janet Dailey

Dani's father had decided that the rough-and-tumble of the race-track was too much for her, and he saw to it that she embarked on a new and very different life under the guidance of Marshall Thompsen. And she might very well have succeeded, if it had not been for her old sparring partner, Barrett King, who insisted on disturbing her new life in more ways than one.

Mills & Boon

SECRETARY WIFE
by Rachel Lindsay

Laura loved her boss, Carl Anderson, but he only saw her as his secretary, and when he became engaged to the beautiful Rosemary, it was Laura whom he asked to help furnish his new home. Then disaster struck Carl and he turned to Laura for help, offering her the chance to become his wife – in order to protect him from the girl he still loved! Should Laura accept him on those terms – and would she ever find happiness if she did?

THE MEDICI LOVER
by Anne Mather

When Suzanne went to Italy for a short holiday with her friend Pietro, she hadn't foreseen that she would fall in love with his forbidding cousin Mazzaro di Falcone. And Mazzaro was an aristocrat, married, with a child – and divorce was out of the question. Was there any solution to Suzanne's problem?

THE WHISPERING GATE
by Mary Wibberley

It was only reluctantly that Andrea had agreed to help Marco Leoni by pretending to be his Uncle Stavros's long-lost granddaughter – but he had persuaded her that it would be an act of kindness to an old man who had not much longer to live. But Marco's formidable cousin Dominic Faro had a very different view of the whole thing – and no opinion at all of Andrea . . .

TIME OF THE TEMPTRESS
by Violet Winspear

Only the tough mercenary Major Wade O'Mara stood between Eve and a singularly unpleasant fate at the hands of African revolutionaries. Thrown together as they were, it was inevitable that Eve should fall in love with Wade. But even if they ever managed to get out of this alive, Wade was a married man, with a son . . .

the rose of romance

ROMANCE

Variety is the spice of romance

Each month, Mills & Boon publish new romances. New stories about people falling in love. A world of variety in romance – from the best writers in the romantic world. Choose from these titles in April.

AN ELUSIVE DESIRE Anne Mather
SUP WITH THE DEVIL Sara Craven
ONE WHO KISSES Marjorie Lewty
ONE MORE TIME Karen van der Zee
A MOUNTAIN FOR LUENDA Essie Summers
PHANTOM MARRIAGE Penny Jordan
CAPTIVE LOVING Carole Mortimer
MASTER OF MORLEY Kay Thorpe
SOMEWHERE TO CALL HOME Kerry Allyne
DARK SEDUCTION Flora Kidd
SECOND TIME AROUND Elizabeth Oldfield
THE TYCOON'S LADY Kay Clifford

On sale where you buy paperbacks. If you require further information or have any difficulty obtaining them, write to: Mills & Boon Reader Service, PO Box 236, Thornton Road, Croydon, Surrey CR9 3RU, England.

Mills & Boon
the rose of romance